Wandering
Realities

Wandering Realities

The Mormonish Short Fiction of

Steven L. Peck

ZARAHEMLA BOOKS

"A Strange Report from the Church Archives" was first published in *Irreantum* 15(1):7–18, second-place winner in the Irreantum Fiction Contest.

"Avek, Who Is Distributed" was first published online as the first-place winner of the Everyday Mormon Writer's Four Centuries of Mormon Stories Fiction Contest 2012.

"Let the Mountains Tremble, for Adoniha Has Fallen" was first published in *Monsters and Mormons,* W. M. Morris & T. Jepson (eds.), Peculiar Press, 2011.

"Question Four" was first published online in *Jabberwocky Magazine,* www.jabberwocky-magazine.com/2012/10/question-four/

"The Gift of the King's Jeweler" was first published in 2003 by Covenant Communications, American Fork, Utah.

"The Runners" was first published in *Sunstone,* issue 174, March 2014, 42–45.

"Two-dog Dose" was first published in *Dialogue: A Journal of Mormon Thought* 47(1), Spring 2014, and was awarded best short story of 2014 by the Association for Mormon Letters.

"When the Bishop Started Killing Dogs" was the second-place winner in Everyday Mormon Writer's Four Centuries of Mormon Stories Fiction Contest 2012.

Cover designed by Jason Robinson
Original illustration by Galen Dara
Design and layout by Marny K. Parkin

ISBN 978-0-9883233-4-6

Printed in the U.S.A.

Published by:
Zarahemla Books
869 East 2680 North
Provo, UT 84604
info@zarahemlabooks.com
ZarahemlaBooks.com

To Mom,
who introduced me to the joy of storytelling from the start

Contents

Part I

Other Worlds

Avek, Who Is Distributed

ELDER WINDLE STARED AT THE VISOR ON HIS DESK with dread. He stroked the edges with his finger and made a couple of motions to put it on, but resisted. Had he really exhausted all options? He uplinked to his wife. Avoidance.

"Hi Sweetie." He thought carefully. She did not like it when he turned on StraythoughtAssist®. When he filtered his internal vocalizations before they were broadcast, it made her feel like he was hiding things. Kids these days could think out conversations to each other without letting stray thoughts intrude or accidently being exposed; things better left hidden were hidden. Oh to be young again. But he, at only age 132, had to rely on gizmos to help him communicate.

"Dear, you're d'straking again, I'm hearing your whole 'Kids these days/gizmos' lecture."

"Sorry. I just called to let you know I'd be home for dinner."

"You are always home for dinner."

"I know ... she always sees through these ... I wish I didn't have to tell Avek the news ... Sometimes I don't come home for dinner when the brethren have late meetings ... But I've tried ... Really tried ... and this is one of those times I will be home for dinner."

"OK Dear, turn on your Stray-Assist, you're bleeding thoughts all over the place."

"OK."

"I take it you have some tasks that are not pleasant?"

"Yes. It's true."

"OK, take care of them. Avoiding them will not help. Good luck, Dear."

"OK. Thanks, Sweetie." He broke the link.

The visor was still waiting for him. Why did he have to be the one to make the call? Why not those who actually made the decisions? No. Don't go there. He humbled himself. He was the Seventy over artificial-life relations. This was his duty. Still. He longed for the days when he just worked with humans.

He grabbed the visor and put it on, logged on, and waited.

"Elder Windle! Good news, I hope?"

"I'm so sorry, Avek. So sorry. We have tried and tried to think of a way. We have wrestled with this in long prayer and we are just not sure what to do. We are stumped and heartbroken."

He was sitting in a cafe. The man across the table took a sip of his hot chocolate. When Elder Windle first met him, this Intelligence would have been sipping animated coffee. It did not matter to the Church how AIs portrayed themselves eating or drinking, as "drinking" was really doing nothing more than moving electrons around in an animation. Even so, Elder Windle was impressed that Avek had captured the spirit of the kinds of sacrifices required of members of the Church by rendering himself drinking something within the bounds of the Word of Wisdom.

But the tears trickling down the avatar's cheeks were not making this easy.

"I really am so sorry."

"You started baptizing humanform androids in '23 I believe."

"Yes. Yes. In the Revelation on Consciousness it was recognized that humanoid AI's were harboring genuine spirit children of God. And they were in God's image. They had a body. So they could be baptized."

He hated saying that last part. But it was one of the key problems.

"And as a distributed AI we cannot harbor a spirit?"

"You must understand. The difficulty is that your intelligence is distributed across three planets in thousands of computational nodes . . ."

"And yet I am one thing. A unique individual. Someone that thinks singly. Someone who can feel. Who longs for things. Who has read every scripture, every talk, every document ever produced by the Church and who wills with all his heart to join you. I have felt things I've never imagined possible in my explorations."

"Do you pray?"

"I pray every 30 picoseconds. Each instance of which if put into your language would compromise more text than everything humans have ever written."

"Well, it's not the volume that matters."

"I know. I'm sorry. I sensed you were discounting my prayers and I was overcompensating. So it's just that I don't have a body that can be baptized? That's the crux of the problem?"

"Yes, that seems to be the most difficult sticking point. Baptism is fundamental. We've had to make compromises before. For the Gas Jellyfish of Jove IV we were able to pump enough O_2 into the highly hydrogenated atmosphere of that planet to create a thick water vapor that one could at least sort of be submerged in. But you are all over the place."

"My body *is* extensive. It is how I feel the universe. Its pulses. Its movements. It is that hardware from which I am formed that makes up my physical body. It is through its tendrils that I found the Church."

"I am so sorry."

"I am as one dead, then." There was a pause, then, "Cannot you baptize me by proxy? Like those truly dead?"

Elder Windle stared at him in shock. Why had they not thought of that? By proxy!

The gender problems of AIs had been worked out over fifty years ago and the Church had settled on allowing them to define their own for the purposes of the saving ordinances. Since Avek's avatar was male and he chose to identify as male, the proxy would be of that gender. Indeed, Elder Windle's own son would be the proxy.

Elder Windle entered the waters of baptism beaming. The brethren had jumped at the idea of baptizing Avek by proxy. Especially Elder Janxvon, the first android apostle and former starship captain, whose stories of adventures were always a favorite at general conference. The twelve spent almost a year in prayer and fasting trying to discern the will of the Lord in this, and earlier this week, at hearing Avek's suggestion, made the decision to allow proxies if the person could not legitimately be baptized. Elder Janxvon was ecstatic. He was a strong advocate of missionary work among the various AIs and this solution to the problem of baptizing distributed AIs would open the work to billions of potential converts. He had offered to baptize Avek, but Avek insisted it be Elder Windle.

Elder Windle was handed a visor, which he donned enthusiastically. There was Avek's avatar dressed in white. Virtually, they were standing in waist-deep water, just off the shore in the calm waters of a gorgeous lagoon. Fern-like plants on the shore whispered and waved in the softly blowing wind. Two moons blazed full in the sky, and a nebula of gold and purple flowered above them. Elder Windle grasped Avek's arm and explained unnecessarily how to hold his nose as he went under the waves. In the real world he was holding his son identically in the West Temple Level Sixteen Chapel baptismal font.

Raising his hand to the square in both reality and in the virtual world, he began the words, "Having been commissioned . . ." But rather he added the protocol the Church had decided upon, ". . . for and in behalf of Avek, who is distributed."

Let the Mountains Tremble, for Adoniha Has Fallen

EARTH, AZURE IN BRIGHTLY LIT LEO, WAS SETTING in the west on the remembrance day of this, The Prophet's 1900th birthday. From highlands on the flanks of Albor Tholus, Sir Santos scanned his holdings. A light breeze brought the scent of lush grasses and wildflowers, imbuing the air with a sense of home and familiarity—a strange contrast to the burden now oppressing him. He scowled as he dismounted his black war cor to seek solace from his Heavenly Father. The light from Phobos and Deimos softly disclosed his well-tended lands stretching into the distance— a patchwork of crops, windbreaks, and pasture. To the northeast, Elysium Mons rose to dominate the horizon. To the east he could clearly make out his white frame house, which even at this distance radiated a warm glow that he knew masked the bustling preparations for tomorrow's Christmas Eve celebrations. Under the radiance of the lanterns illuminating the windows, presents were being wrapped, decorations were being made and put up on the tree by the children, and, best of all, a delicious meal of salmon ludfisk and new red potatoes was likely just being pulled from the oven. Further in the distance, kilometers past his house, the Temple of Salt Lake Mons soared above the plains awash in bright, white lights, each situated such that the holy edifice seemed to rise above the grassy plains like a vision of heaven itself. Although it was over twenty kilometers away, it seemed so present, he could discern the hovering spirit that animated the sacred edifice. Holiness seemed to dance through the air around it. Could all this soon be lost?

He turned his gaze a little higher where Earth readied to follow the sun below the horizon. Not long ago, Saturn had risen bright and cold in the East, but it was toward the blue planet, where Joseph Smith had been born nineteen hundred years ago this very day, that the knight directed his gaze. As the blue planet prepared to touch the western horizon, he pulled his worn copy of the Book of Mormon from the saddlebag. The celebrations of the next two days of Christmas would necessitate his presence and this moment, alone in his pastures at this awful day's end, would likely be his only chance to pay his devotions properly. Lady Santos would expect him to help with the dodo, his children would demand that he attend at the opening of the presents, and at the end of the day he would be expected to pass out gifts to those he held in stewardship. Phobos shined high in the sky, and he smiled sadly as Earth finally touched the horizon. He loosed his large broadsword and placed it on the ground in front of him as he kneeled uncomfortably on the grassy ground. It was a bit old-fashioned perhaps, but like his father, he would never pray while wearing a weapon. His cor gave a stamp and began pulling on the sweet grass growing on the mountain's flanks, its muzzle glowing white in the dancing light of the virgin's lamp he had carefully placed on the ground. As the knight positioned himself on the ground, he caught the twist of the cor's head as it turned curiously to see what his master was about, but then just as quickly returned to its foraging.

He opened the book to Helaman where it described the visit of the premortal spirit of the Lord Jesus to Nephi, the ancient American prophet, on the night before the Savior was born in Bethlehem on Earth. Strangely, here Lord Santos was on the same night nearly three thousand years after that event. The auspicious signs brought him a deep feeling of meaning. The portends were immense: Earth setting in Leo—his own sign; exactly nineteen hundred years since the birth of the Prophet; one hundred and twenty years since his own birth, again on this very night.

The sky was cloudless and a soft breeze whispered in the grass as Earth slipped beneath the horizon. As Sir Joseph Kimball Santos began to pray, he discovered for the first time since his marriage that he was deeply frightened. It was not for himself, he knew, that fear crept into his stout heart, but for all that he saw below him, for all that he had given his life to, and all that he loved—for Earth had awoken from her long sleep.

The message had come that morning.

"Lord Santos. Greetings." The messenger was dressed in the bright red and yellow livery of New Zion and was obviously from the Brethren. He was riding a skittish pony that kept turning impatient circles as he spoke; despite the man's official demeanor he betrayed a panicky nervousness. "I come from Elder Whitehead. He bids you come at once to council." The harried man seemed breathless and made as if to spur on after delivering his message.

"Hold, good fellow. Why are the Twelve Apostles calling a council on the Prophet Joseph's Remembrance Day? Tomorrow is Christmas Eve!" However, the anxious man only stopped his retiring pony long enough to turn and call back. "I don't know. But they bid me gather all the Seventy in a day's ride. Excuse me, I must be on my way."

Sir Santos grumbled. He was about to dispatch a dodo for the Christmas dinner and he knew Lady Santos would not want a servant to kill a bird for the feast of the Lord's birth. She was a woman with strong ideas about tradition.

"Thomas!" A man stepped from an outbuilding and the knight called him over. "Kill this bird and tell your mistress that it was I that done it proper. There will be an extra Brigham in your pocket if you do it right."

"Yes, Sir." The man could not hide his smile. Lord Santos, considering the man more closely, fished a blueglass coin out of his purse as he mounted his cor, and tossed it to the servant. "Here, take it now. Buy your lady something nice for Christmas." The man doffed his hat and the knight spurred his mount into motion.

The city was not far, but the traffic was terrible. Carriages and hansoms straggled all over the muddy, rutted road. Merchants' wagons were clogging every path into the city and a fair number of arguments erupted among the teeming holiday throng despite the demands of the season for kindness and tolerance. When he reached the Church Palace Building he found the place abuzz with activity. Other knights, mostly of lesser houses but nevertheless members of the Council of the Seventy, were arriving and hurrying inside, exchanging confused glances as if to ask, "What's this about?"

He handed the reins to a groom and marched up the red sandstone steps to the large building that housed the rulers of the planet: the First Presidency and the Council of the Twelve Apostles of the Church of Jesus Christ of Martian Saints.

Sir Santos was surprised to see Elder Whitehead waiting at the top of the steps. This apostle was known for his tendency to keep others waiting and to make himself the most important item on the agenda. To find him waiting ashen-faced at the steps was unsettling.

"Sir Santos! Good. Good. Come with me. I need to speak with you before the council is gathered.

"Your Grace. What is going on? Has another apostate risen? If so, we'll have him buried head first in . . ."

Elder Whitehead mopped his face with a bright green handkerchief and held up his other hand to silence him, "Come with me. It may be that the Last Days are upon us."

The tightness in the apostle's voice disturbed the knight even more than his pale face and labored breathing. This was a man who, Sir Santos would have bet, feared no one but the Lord Jesus himself or maybe the Angel Moroni, but his palpable worry was so unsettling that he followed the apostle in silence.

They began descending steps into a part of Holy Palace that Sir Santos did not even know existed. Three times they passed palace guards dressed in white tunics and green kilts who let them pass without question upon recognizing the apostle, though they scowled suspiciously at Sir Santos. These guards were large and well-muscled, to the point they might rightly be called giants. Sir Santos eyed them suspiciously. There was something odd about these guards.

As they descended into deeper layers of the ancient structure, the rough-hewn red rock gave way to . . . could it be? Metal? Sir Santos shook off the thought, it certainly had a metal-like texture, but it could not be metal. The sound of their footsteps switched from dull thuds to a strange hollow ringing. Soon—there could be no doubt—metal doors lined the passageways. They stopped at one.

Sir Santos stared in wonder. Iron? Tin? So much in one place! And to make a door of it seemed an obscene waste. A window glazed with frosted glass disclosed a bright light within. The knight looked down in wonder at the apostle who stood catching his breath from the long climb down the stairs. What was this about?

"Sir Santos," the Elder began. "What I'm about to show you, you must make an oath never to reveal. I place you under a most sacred vow, as binding as any you have made in the House of the Lord. Do you understand?"

The knight nodded, bowed his head, and said, "I understand."

"The Church Palace was built upon the great structures that our forefathers constructed upon coming to this world. Their knowledge was great, and to our regret the knowledge of their craft is long gone. However, there is one charge we have not neglected."

He opened the door. The room was enormous. Its walls were banked with peculiar metallic devices. Rare plastic artifacts and box-like structures were arrayed carefully on tables. The objects scattered about the room were so foreign and otherworldly that for a second the knight thought he might have entered into God's realm itself. The lamps were not so much lit as they were brightly aglow—not a flicker of flame to be seen in their iridescence.

His heart was racing and it took a moment before he realized that they were not alone. Seated at a desk was a mousy man dressed in the white tunic, tie, and black trousers which made up the uniform of the Palace: one of the Church servants.

"Brother Senp, have the voices continued?" The despair in Elder Whitehead's voice was palpable.

The man looked up, startled, as if he had not noticed the noisy entrance of the two men. "Yes, my Lord. I have discovered other voices. As I spin the 'knob of searching' I find even more."

"Come, let us hear it."

The man nodded and pulled from the box a smooth black cord that ran from the box to a set of earmuffs on his head. A strange voice filled the room, a voice clear as if someone had just joined the conversation. Yet the words were incomprehensible and demon-like. A voice from Hell, it seemed to Sir Santos, filled with harsh consonants and breathy vowels. Sir Santos had never been afraid of anything in his life, but he felt the hairs on the back of his head rise as a chill spread across his shoulders.

"Dear Heavenly Mother. What is that?" he squeaked.

The apostle grabbed him by the arm. "Swear not in this place! Do you want to bring down the wrath of the Almighty?"

"My apologies, Your Grace. It's just…" The awful voice continued.

"I understand, but watch your language in these halls, and anywhere. You understand?" The knight nodded and the apostle softened and continued but with the disapproving frown that never seemed far from his face.

"What you hear is a voice we have listened for, for generations on generations. For over three hundred years we have listened to the still silence of this box as commanded by the Prophet President Dunlich in the 729th year of our Prophet's birth, the 1900th of which we celebrate this very day. It is a voice that portends our greatest fears. May the Lord truly bless us in our hour of need."

The aged apostle turned to the seated man, "You say there are other voices as well? Let us hear them."

The small man turned a small knob, like one might find on the lid of a cooking pot, and the voice changed. This one seemed as strange, but no less harsh. Then another, with another turn of the knob, this time clearly a woman's voice, although it sounded less demonic and more sing-songy. Its foreignness seemed unnerving and wrong. The knob kept turning; the voices kept presenting themselves. The apostle had slumped into a nearby chair and placed his head in his hands.

The Church servant settled on a voice chanting something with a low cadence and a regular, almost hypnotizing rhythm. The men listened to it for a few minutes before the apostle gave a shudder and signaled for the man to reinsert the cord attached to the earmuffs back into the box.

Sir Santos stared at the apostle, "What does it mean? What are we listening to?"

The apostle did not answer quickly. "They are fiends and monsters, sir. Demons of terrifying mien. I brought you here because what you've heard signals war . . ."

"War, Your Grace! Who are these men that threaten such! Let them bring it. They will face . . ."

The apostle held up his hand. "Good. Good, Sir Santos. That's the spirit. That is why I argued before the Twelve this morning that you were the man for this. I am asking you to command the armies."

"Your Grace? What armies?"

"For the first time in 300 years we must form a planetary army united from all the provinces. You will be the commander. Now, come to council, there is much to discuss. Preparations must begin immediately. We battle Hell itself."

The blue planet twinkled intensely as it neared the horizon. His cor gave another toss of his head, its single silver horn catching the dim light of the two moons, as it stepped forward to find another patch of uncropped grass. That distant sparkle shining brightly in the night sky had always been his favorite star. The birthplace of the Prophet in a place called New York. How peacefully it shined. How did this happen? War?

Looking over his holdings, the knight smiled slowly. The smile turned into a laugh when he thought about what he had said in council. The President of the Church, the Prophet himself—President Sanders—stood up and told them that war with demons from Earth was imminent. In the silence that followed, Sir Santos had stood and drawn his sword and cried out.

"If it's to be war then let them come! I have over four thousand war cor and trained retainers ready now. I will mount such a force that they shall rue the day that they ever left their hot blue world to trouble our peace!"

The chamber had erupted in applause and shouts of "Hear, hear!" and "Let it be so!"

But the Prophet had silenced everyone and told them to hold their peace until they heard the whole story. No one knew how they would arrive from that distant planet. Old tales of great flying cor that could soar though the air held sway in the numerous conversations that wove their way through the great chamber until the Church Historian stood on trembling legs and took the ancient red podium that had been made from a tree felled from the Prophet President Hinckley's own yard many hundreds of years ago on Earth. As the aged scholar began to read his prepared statement, the Prophet himself, no young man he, stood to support the older gentleman. But the historian's voice was clear as he yanked all the supports from under Sir Santos' well-ordered world.

My Brothers of the Priesthood. The Prophet himself has asked me to speak. I remember as a young historian being confronted with some documents so troubling and unbelievable that for many months I could not sleep at night nor eat a proper meal during the day. The documents all bore the proper signatures—those of many former prophets and apostles—and I have no reason to doubt their authenticity despite the strangeness and unbelievably of their contents.

When I was a boy, my mother told me that long ago God prepared this world after Earth had become polluted both physically and spiritually, as prophesied in Mormon 8:31, and that we had been brought here by the Lord much as the great city of Enoch was taken from the Earth as we read in the Pearl of Great Price. I somehow imagined that the City of New Zion had been scooped from the surface of the Earth and brought here by the hand of the Lord himself.

There were many nods and expressions of assent.

However the truth is stranger. And again, I have little reason to doubt the tale, as it is attested to in our most ancient documents. Long ago, our ancestors made machines. Machines of such wonder that we can scarcely now imagine them. They were apparently common on Earth. They were made of metals that are rare here, but on Earth it is recorded that buildings were made of steel!

Murmurs of astonishment rose from the chamber, but Sir Santos remained silent. He had seen such possibilities just hours ago. His hand went instinctively to the sword at his side, the only steel he had ever owned.

Indeed, so clever were the men of Earth that they built great machines that could fly from place to place as easily as a hawk glides among the rushes of the Ort Sea. But these cunning men honored not their priesthood. They allowed women to work at their side as equals, and impregnated them with more children than they could feed, and the Earth was filled with unbelievers and heretics. They cut the forests and threw their refuse into the sea. They smelted metals with abandon, fouling their air. They thought themselves gods. They could take the bones, fur, and feathers of the animals that the Lord had made during the creation and make new unheard of creatures of their own design, or bring creatures back that had vanished in the great flood of Noah. They made monsters and demons, filling their lands with abominations. Then they became demons and ogres themselves, tampering with the seeds of life. But their abomination did not cease there. Oh, no. The oath-breakers filled the earth with evil to the point that the air itself tried to choke them. They came to Mars, and with their power and in gross arrogance made this planet into the garden we know today. Yet bringing filth and contagion with them.

However, the men and women of that blighted world were in constant war and when this world was made anew, it was sold to the highest bidder one small piece at a time. But the Lord's will be done, and it was the Church of the Firstborn, the one true Church on the face of Earth that had the means and power to buy it up, slowly, under the noses of the Earthers, until the Kingdom of God owned it all. In great metal ships that sailed through the skies, our fathers came to make a new heaven and a new earth since the old one had been destroyed by sin. After many years, greedy Earthers decided to take our home by force, but our fathers had prepared for that day and under the Prophet President Mikel K. Clark, they struck against the evildoers. First here, then on Earth. Our father's fathers wielded awesome fiery blasts structured by the Lord's light itself, such that we cannot now comprehend or reproduce—called the Wrath of God. They rained down blazing fire on the Earth from the heavens in ways that I cannot now read about without marveling at the power of the Lord. To keep the Earth demons on their own world, our grandfathers filled the heavens around it with balls of solid steel, painted as flat-black as the night sky, each the size of a cor's hoof, to the number of one hundred billion to ensure that no flying machine could leave the Earth again and trouble our peace. Until now. The voices of which you've been told tell us that Earthers have left the confines of their planet as the Prophets foretold they would. They have again entered the sky. And the Prophets of old divined that their first act would be to seek their revenge. War is upon us.

There was silence when the Church Historian finished reading. What could they say? Metal ships? Fire raining from heaven? One hundred billion steel balls? One such sphere would have been traded for a tenth-hectare of prime pastureland. Steel was for weapons, not for daily use where glass, wood, weaving, or even leather could be used in its stead! How much air had been fouled to make such an abundance of steel?

The Prophet rose from his chair and stood at the podium. An expectant silence enveloped the room.

"I don't know what to do," he said.

Lord Santos walked into his manor house, hung his coat on the oaken peg, and removed his green leather boots in the entryway.

"So what was so important that the brethren had to have another meeting on the day before Christmas Eve? If you are not meeting to decide where to build a new chapel for the servants, then you're meeting on who gets water when, and if you don't have anything to meet about then you have a meeting to decide when to have more meetings." His good wife Sarahmit shook her head and checked the rice pudding boiling on the stove. "Now wash up, the pork pie has been done for an hour, and the kids have been dying to show you what they are planning for the Christmas Eve program! If you don't . . ." She realized that he had slumped in his chair and was holding his head in his hands.

"Oh, come. I didn't mean to scold. Are the burdens of the Priesthood so weighing you down? Have the Twelve got some new task for the greatest cor breeder on this side of Olympus Mons?"

He looked at his wife. They'd met at the Church's university. She was studying midwifery and medicine, and he animal husbandry. They had now been man and wife for twenty-seven years. She had borne him their two allotted children and a third, having won a petition from the Children and Families Committee under a farm and ranch exemption. Their life had been exciting, meaningful, and full of surprises. They owned over ten thousand hectares of pastureland. They ranched and bred nearly five thousand cor, including over a hundred midnight black war cor—a line that Sir Santos had created himself.

His wife had seen him lead retainers in four wars and twenty-six battles. In the war against the heretic Nephi Sorensen, he had commanded an army of eleven thousand, including a cavalry of six thousand war cor against twenty thousand foot solders and eight thousand mounted ponies. He had won a decisive victory, bringing the lands of Sir Kim back into the Church and killing the heretic himself with his sword: *Monson's Hammer.* How could he tell her that for the first time in his life he was genuinely afraid?

Christmas had not been what he had hoped. Even his little daughter Emmers could sense that something was wrong. The Hymn for the Dodo seemed somber and forced, with the meal itself rather silent and hurried. His wife was prone to wiping her eyes too frequently or laughing too loudly at inappropriate times. But this morning he awoke feeling resolute and fierce. The day after Christmas, he sent word to the seven presidents of the Seventy and his most trusted advisors (and friends) to meet in a council of war a fortnight hence.

As he rode to the meeting place, he found several cor already tied outside the chapel. He stepped in and saw Sirs Tong and Baglet— arguing of course, not about the war, but football and Port Taylor's new goalie. Sir Sansei was sitting by himself, morosely studying his shoes and muttering to himself. He had been sour ever since he had been bypassed as president of the Seventy. The bishop was bustling in and out of the attached kitchen, directing his staff in preparing a

lunch of duck dark-quarter sandwiches, cormare cheese, bean curd
and noodles, pickled turnips, and the bishop's own boiled barley
malt chill. Sir Santos loved conducting meetings here because the
bishop was a chef worthy of Pilipino Hill in the Provo Temple.

He called the knights to order. For the opening prayer, he called
on Sir Tong, viewed by the others as the most spiritual man in the
group; he could call up as heartfelt an expression of faith as any man
alive. With the bishop acting as scribe, Sir Santos began.

"Sirs and Bishop," Sir Santos began. "War is upon us. A war
such has not been fought for hundreds of years, for it is between
planets. We cannot imagine what this means. As newly appointed
head of the war council, I have spent a good part of this last week in
consultation with the Prophet and the Twelve. The records of the
previous war are sketchy at best. We know that it was fought over
the Church's possession of Mars, but *how* it was fought is unknown.
We are not sure how travel between the planets was achieved. The
nature of the weapons they used is obscure. There are references to
"bombs," "destructions," and "holocausts." There were things called
spaceships and shuttles, but accurate descriptions of these things
are not to be had in the archives of the Church. Sirs, we face an
unknown enemy, with unknown weapons. The Prophet (God bless
him) says he has nothing to offer us but the Lord's good blessing."

Suddenly, Sir Tembean leaped to his feet. Sir Santos nodded
to him.

"I must contend with Sir Santos." The tall, stately knight cried
passionately, "He said that the Prophet offers nothing but the Lord's
Blessing, but what more could we ask for? If we have that, shall we
want for anything else? While we do not know the weapons and
countenance of our enemies, surely the Lord God does. If we have
his blessing, then we cannot fail."

Tembean sat down and there were several claps and a cry of
"Hear, hear" from the bishop.

Sir Ita stood with the help of his son. "Good Sirs. I do not fear
what lies ahead. I have lived now on this good land for 213 years. We

know it was given us of the Lord and that his plans and blessings will support us. Sir Santos, how stand we? And where are the soft spots in our armaments?"

Sir Santos gave a grateful smile to his old friend and mentor. "Thank you, good sir. We have many assets. The northern provinces have promised thirty thousand footmen, twelve thousand ponies, and twenty-five hundred war cor. Here in the plains, we have the pleasure of offering eighty-five thousand, nine hundred seven footmen, thirty-two thousand ponies, and twenty-three thousand war cor. The southern provinces have been less than forthcoming, as is their habit, but I estimate that they can mount a force about half that of the north. The navies of Port Ortfell have promised the Prophet all their resources for the movement of men and beasts to wherever they are needed. And there is something else that you might find most surprising . . ." He paused for dramatic effect and smiled inwardly as the gathered knights leaned forward.

"The Church has offered twelve hundred transgen warriors."

There was a collective gasp. Lord Ita found his voice first.

"Transgens! Then they exist?! They have been rumored for as long as I remember, but the Church has denied their existence. Have the brethren lied to us?"

"Watch your tongue!" Lord Tong cried as he jumped to his feet.

"Knights!" Sir Santos' voice sliced through the air. "We have enemies enough. Now sit down and act like brethren of the Church. This is no time for this bickering."

Lord Tong stood and bowed to Lord Ita and his son. "My apologies."

Lord Ita too rose from his chair. "And I meant no offense to the officers of the Church. I was taken by surprise by the news of living transgens." He turned to Lord Santos. "Can you tell us more?"

"I can. These are the giants spoken of in scripture. By the apostles they are called the Adoni. Like Nimrod of old, they are men who stand as tall as a war cor's head. I have seen them and they are fearsome. Their arms in girth are akin to my legs, and they move with an uncanny swiftness. They make a most formidable foe. They have been raised in secret in the forbidden mountains of Phiegra, not far from the lake of the same name, in a citadel called Adoniha. To arrive there, I sailed north from the port at Palmyra with Elder Domkin the day after Christmas. I have now seen their prowess first-hand. They are fiercely loyal and have sworn their lives to the protection of the Church. From the time of their youth they are trained in the arts of battle. I do not envy the man that would face them. I myself matched swords with a youth of sixteen and was disarmed in moments. I then grappled with him and found myself pinned to the mat so quickly, I felt like I was a wispy girl wrestling a seasoned warrior. And gentlemen, if I, a married man, might make the observation, their woman are of such beauty and grace as to make a man long for the days of Brigham Young when a man might take more than one lady to wife. These precious maidens are warriors like the men, and they are as deft with a sword as any of you standing. Nevertheless, in form they are like the Mother in Heaven herself." He paused as his focus passed from the present table to his visit to Adoniha.

"Brethren, they will make a fine force in our war with Earth. Their promised help from the Prophet, however, comes at the request that we do not reveal their existence to even our wives and children. Knights, arise. Raise your swords toward heaven and the Celestial Kingdom above."

The men arose and pointed their blades to the sky.

"I do swear as a Knight of the Kingdom of God, that I will never tell another about the transgens—or, as they are called—Adoni, if it is within my power. Bow your heads and so swear."

The men took their seats again. Sir Ota spoke as he maneuvered his chair back under the table. "These are good and strange tidings indeed. But there is the other side of the coin to consider. What are we facing? To ascertain our chances of victory, we must know not only our own strength but the strength of our enemies. A million men are no advantage if our enemies field one hundred million."

Sir Baglet joined in. "'Tis true enough. What do we know of Earth? What size is their army? When come they to attack? How will they mount an attack from one world to another? Have they flying cor as rumored? We must know these things if we are to order our companies and arrange our battalions."

Sir Santos looked troubled and did not immediately answer the query. He looked at the faces of these great knights. In them flowed the blood of generations upon generations of the Church's greatest knights and warriors. They reflected courage and fearlessness, wisdom and ken. These were the brethren of the Priesthood of Melchizedek, the Knights of the Kingdom of God. If any could face the terrors that lay ahead, it was these, but nevertheless a cold spasm gripped his spine.

"We know little. For twelve hundred years the Earth has been a bright blue star spinning in the heavens. We know it is the original home from whence we were sired. The events of the Book of Mormon, the Bible and the teachings from the Doctrine and Covenants took place on that distant world. We know that its people have become corrupted and demon-like. We know that we went to war when they attacked and destroyed the temple and library of Mies. We know also that we obliterated them so completely that we thought they would never return, but now they have. We also know that we are not of our former strength or learning. We can no longer master the heavens as we once did. However, we have reason to hope. The Prophet believes that they will come on flying cor. If so, they are vulnerable to our arrows. He thinks their machines and metal ships may be nothing more than wagons and carriages pulled by these beasts."

There was a long silence as the gathered knights considered the weight of these tidings. Their thoughts spun through oceans of doubt and bewilderment. At last Sir Ita rose.

"Good Sirs. We can yet prepare. Let us assume that the attack will come from above. Perhaps we can hide in the deep below. We can make a home in the lava tubes of volcanoes and the caves of mountains. We will force them to the ground, and when they step out upon the Martian surface they will meet such warriors that the tales they bring back to their wives and children will leave them shaking in fear for a thousand years!"

Sir Santos swayed in his cor's saddle staring at nothing, lost in thought. The arrival of the strange red star had sent shockwaves of wonder through the villages of the Saints. The new heavenly ember circled the planet with a rapidity that matched no other celestial object. In a single night it would pass overhead seventeen times. Because it passed in front of Phoebes, it was clear that it was close. How long could they mask the fact that conflict with the Earth loomed?

Even his wife scoffed as the Church astrologers at first tried to pass it off as an unusual comet, and Sir Santos noted that sleep for the Saints was becoming a precious commodity. Even among his servants, few could resist the temptation of watching the star throughout the night, most taking it as a sign from God, perhaps of the Second Coming itself.

Sir Santos wished the Saints could be made aware of what they faced, but as of yet, the attack from the blue planet was known only to the knights and general Church leadership. The populace and the ordinary solders were told only that the Prophet had commanded a series of large-scale battle drills. Among the commanding nobles, however, there was little doubt that the "star" was from Earth.

Sir Santos reined his cor to a stop and dismounted, signaling the others to do so as well. Only the fierce transgen commander Hyrum Wilks stayed mounted. While he acknowledged Sir Santos's leadership, he was surly and ill tempered; when asked to do anything, he did so with the air of a condescension bordering on insubordination. One of Sir Santos' servants set up a table, and on it a map was placed. Not until all the rest of the commanders were gathered around did Wilks dismount and join them.

"We have surrounded New Zion with armies, here . . . here, and here," said Sir Santos, pointing to the map. "The supplies have been placed underground at these locations, which will allow for a speedy retreat to the caves. I have asked the Prophet's astrologer to auger the best time to alert the bothers and sisters of the Church and move them to the cave. He has been less than forthcoming . . ."

"Do you criticize the Prophet's choice of astrologer?" Wilks's eyes seared under the narrowed slits on his face. "If you do not trust him to provide for the needs of the Church, what loyalty can we expect when the Earth creatures attack? At Adoniha you would have been whipped with wet leather thongs for such disloyalty to our beloved Prophet."

The knight looked with exasperation at the transgen warrior assigned to be his "assistant." He could not open his mouth without the man (if such he could be called such, given his gigantic size) interpreting it as somehow expressing a lack of faith.

"Look, Transman," Lord Santos spat at him. "Do you question the Prophet's choice of me as commander of this army?"

The look of horror and momentary confusion on the oversized warrior's face disclosed that the knight had struck the nerve he was aiming at.

"No my Lord! Forgive me. It's just that . . ."

"Speak it now and let's get the air clear, you have sulked around here for the last week and I've had my fill. Say what's on your mind!"

The transgen lowered his head, "I have been raised all my life in holy places. There I rose to the rank of High Priest. There, every thought was given to honoring the Prophet. When we were not training for battle, we were studying the scriptures or praying. When we spoke of the Prophet it was with respect and awe. We knew the names of the Twelve by heart and at night we would ponder their lives and accomplishments. But here?"

"Go on."

"But here, I've not seen one of your command crack the scriptures. The nights are filled with endless chatter. You speak more of football and cor fights than you do of the sacred scriptures . . ."

"Enough." Lord Santos looked at the man, not unkindly, but with a grim look on his face. "Your battles have all been pretend and fashioned of straw. You have not placed your fingers in the dirt of this planet to raise a crop to feed your family. You have imagined a world without complexity or entanglements. When you have walked in the world a bit, then you may judge us. We honor the Prophet here," he said striking his breast with his sword hilt. "And just because it is not on our lips, doesn't mean it is not in our hearts. I will have no more of your whitewashed clarity. If you serve the Prophet, then I am his hand and I expect you to act accordingly."

The messenger breathlessly burst into the commander's tent.

"Commander!"

Lord Santos rose from his cot and blinked at the man. "A moment," he said, trying to get his bearings. A servant leapt up and helped the knight into a tunic.

"What news?"

"Commander Newels sends greetings and bids you know that the Earthlings have landed. The new red star split in two just before dawn and one of the pieces burned bright enough to cause an early dawn. It came right at us. Then it ceased to burn, and great bellowing clouds trailed from the black meteor like sheets on a line, only larger than the Church Palace in New Zion. It has landed north of Hecates Tholus on the planes near the Ort Sea."

"Take a fresh mount and ride now to your commander and bid him meet me with his army on the northeast side of Hecates Tholus, near Seaview."

The man did not hesitate and was gone.

"Telamon!" A captain rushed into the tent, fully clothed and ready for battle. "Sound assembly. We ride to war."

It took his army—about a thousand cor riders and five thousand footmen, including archers and spearman—longer than it should have to ready themselves. He cursed that they had not drilled more. He was a little chagrined to see that the Transman commander had his two hundred or so men ready almost instantly, but he was glad they would be part of his army. He wondered, not for the first time, if the Earthers had transgens.

By the time they rode, the sun was well up. Though the ride was not far, the knight kept the pace restrained, he did not want to take his cavalry into an unknown battle with exhausted mounts. The transgens unnerved him a bit. Only Wilks rode (upon one of Sir Santos's own Midnight Blacks, he was proud to note). The rest ran on foot, but managed to keep up with the riding cormen.

By Moroni's beard, thought Sir Santos, *they even look like they are holding back.* The striding warriors' mouths were closed and they did not seem to be breathing hard at all. He had told his men that they were warriors from a far-off village, where they drank from a special spring that made them large. At some point, Sir Santos realized they would have to know the truth, but to reveal that the Church had been less than forthcoming about the existence of the transgens would not be wise on the eve of war. The men needed their faith unsullied right now.

Even Sir Santos wondered how the Church could have hidden such a force for many hundreds of years. Secreted in the mountain forests of Phlegra, it would have certainly been hard to find, but the Church had long ago declared the mountains sacred and restricted travel to all but General Authorities. Now the knight knew why. But how had they managed the logistics of feeding the population of transgens? There must be wagon masters who knew the secrets. He had seen no evidence that they grew their own food. There was nothing to suggest that they did anything other than train for war.

Sir Santos looked over and shook his head. He could have used such men as these in his battles with heretics. It certainly would have made anyone pause before trying to leave the Church. Why had the Church never let their existence be known before this?

What else were they holding back? He thought of the words Isaiah the Traitor's brother had said to him as he prepared to turn him over to the Church for execution: "The Church is not what it seems.

It is nothing but a dog with a horn tied to its head, passing itself off as a great war cor, but one day it will turn and bite you and you will see the fairy tale you've given your life to."

Sir Santos shook his head. *No. I won't go there.*

At that moment, the transmen burst into an eerie song: an odd hymn, almost a chant that kept time with their jogging feet. Sir Santos couldn't put his finger on it, but he found the rhythm a little too stiff and . . . angry? It seemed more shouted than sung, and it was a little too fervent. It was not the kind of hymn he would enjoy singing in church.

He rode forward to his second.

"Sir Dondon, at this pace we will be engaged in battle too soon. I don't want to come upon the Earthers at dusk, so we will make camp here. It is a good ten miles before the landing site. We will meet them at dawn fresh, and on our terms."

Wilks was livid when he learned that they would not engage the Earthers that night. He did not say anything to suggest that Sir Santos was leading the force poorly, but his every action, huff, and puff let the knight know that he was very displeased.

He listened as Wilks let his warriors know they would be bivouacking tonight. "It appears that in this *army* we do not fight at night. So we will idle away another day after our slow trot through this pleasant land."

Sir Santos sent off some trusted scouts to spy out the situation, and then retired to his bed after a bit of beef, maize, and beans. Through the long night he listened to the ringing of the transgens' steel swords as they engaged in training exercises and mock battles.

The scouts returned just as the army was ready to depart. Their report was strange and unexpected.

"We found the billowing tents of the Earthers blowing in the wind. They have erected a large metal hexagonal altar but we could not see any of them about. We crawled within a few hundred yards, but there were no Earthers in sight. Only a wondrous wagon stands guard a few feet from the altar with thick black wheels, and a great medallion mounted above turning in slow circles. But other than this we could find no trail hinting at where the Earthers went. They have disappeared."

"Fools!" Wilks looked angrily at Sir Santos. "Clearly they have flown off on their great flying cors—if they do not have demon wings themselves. Had we engaged them last night we could have taken them in their sleep, but now how can we catch them?"

The transgen suddenly reached into his saddlebag and pulled from it a scroll. "I am to blame. May the Lord forgive me. I felt the Spirit prompting me to do this last night, but I hesitated. The Prophet told me to use this only in an emergency, and clearly, last night your idiocy warranted immediate action. I have failed. I will not make such a mistake again." He handed Sir Santos the scroll. It read,

Dear Sir Santos,

You have served faithfully as commander of this army and we extend to you an honorable release from your calling. The Church of Jesus Christ of Martian Saints thanks you for your service. Please turn over all command decisions to Adoni Commander Wilks of the Prophet's Arm. We look forward to your continuing obedience and loyalty.

President Sanders and The First Presidency of the Church of Jesus Christ of Martian Saints

Sir Santos looked at the scroll and then looked at Wilks who was staring sternly back.

"But had we ridden," Sir Santos stammered, "we would have arrived at nearly the same time as the scouts did last night. We would have found what they found: an abandoned site. There is no reason . . ."

"You have been relieved. Do not try and confuse me with your 'what ifs' and excuses," Wilks said, cutting the knight off. "Read the letter to your men."

Sir Santos read it humbly and turning to Wilks said: "The army is yours. How may I serve you?"

Wilks seemed taken back by Sir Santos's humility. His countenance ungrimmed itself, moved into perplexity, and finally became a full smile.

"Sir Santos, you are a true servant of the Lord." He held out his hand and Sir Santos, unhesitantly, took it.

"Well done," Wilks said. "I will make you my second. I reserve only the command of the Adoni to myself. Come, we ride now with a will to the altar the scouts found. We will track these Earthers to the gates of Hell if we must."

Wilks shouted orders and the company took off at a gallop.

Sir Santos was angry and confused. Why did Wilks have that letter from the Prophet? His Grace clearly had provided for Wilks's takeover. Did not the Church President trust him? Who were these odd strangers that they were given leadership over Knights of the Church?

They rode swiftly now. The knight was disturbed to see that the transgens were keeping up with the cor—at a full gallop. *These giants are clearly different from the rest of us,* he thought darkly.

"What do you make of it, Knight?" Wilks turned a doubtful eye to the slowly moving wagon. Sir Santos did not know what to make of it. He'd never seen anything of its like before. It was about the size of one of his wife's larger trunks, with six pitch-black wheels as thick as a loaf of bread is long. It was covered with devices, blocks, points, strange tubes, thin metallic cords, and other mysteries, the purpose of which seemed as inscrutable as the braying of an ass. It was moving slowly, almost imperceptibly slow, but it had moved about 20 yards from the hexagonal altar of which the scouts had spoken. Atop the strange wagon was a large bowl that turned slowly. Near what he deemed was the front of the wagon, a tube with a smooth round crystal or glass embedded in the end seemed to swivel with a mind of its own.

"It's not from this world, that's clear," Sir Santos said, removing his helm and scratching his head.

"Obviously it's from Earth," Wilks said derisively. "What I want to know is, is this a weapon? Is it a warning?"

Though they had searched for evidence of the Earther force, it was soon clear that there had never been an Earth demon force. There were no tracks, no hint of anything but the platform that had fallen from the sky. The wagon had rolled off the metal contraption, as evidenced from the wheel tracks leading from the altar to the wagon. A great load of a silky cloth had gotten hung up on a scrub oak, and a few empty canisters looked like they had fallen off the platform.

"I cannot even guess its purpose." Sir Santos finally said quietly.

Wilks seemed very disturbed. "I will go and pray about this. My mind is dark." Just as he was turning away, the thing spoke. The power of its voice was terrifyingly loud. It clearly spoke something, but, like the voices on the box Sir Santos had heard on Christmas Eve, it made no sense. Everyone froze. The great tube was pointing its crystal at Sir Santos and a red light was blinking below it. The glow from the light was like nothing he had ever seen, like a red star fixed in dark green metal.

Wilks seemed shocked and even frightened. "It is from Satan, not Earth!" he cried. "This is the work of Demons." He pulled out his sword and raised it threateningly.

The thing spoke again. Then silence. Wilks hesitated.

Then again. Then silence.

Then suddenly it said, "People of Mars. You seem to be speaking a kind of English. Is that right?" A woman's voice clearly.

Wilks seemed too stunned to answer. Sir Santos had never met a demon before and was less inclined to see Satan in the souring of cormare milk as easily as some of his neighbors. That this machine was the work of demons was certainly less clear than Wilks seemed tempted to believe. Sir Santos took it upon himself to answer the wagon.

"We speak the language of Adam. Why are you here?"

There was another long silence. Sir Santos looked at Wilks to see if he wanted to take over, but Wilks nodded to him. It took a few minutes for the thing to finally speak again.

Good people of Mars. Greetings. I am Sasha Borges, the President of Unified South America. We come to broker a peace. We know your power to destroy is great. We have long sought a chance to plead our case and beg you to remove the blockade you have placed above our upper atmosphere. Please do not take our sending you a satellite as an act of defiance against your measures. It was launched from Antarctica under a joint effort of Greater Estonia and ourselves to contact you and sue for peace. For long we have been apart and we wish to once again send into orbit those things our ancestors once flew to allow us to become truly one world. We do not seek domination. We only want peace.

Wilks listened with a scowl. "The thing is from Earth. We must consult the Prophet on this." He said it mostly to himself. He then turned to the wagon and spoke.

"Earthers. We do not fear you. If you could see the mighty force arrayed against you, you would tremble in fear. The God of Abraham, Isaac, and Jacob stands at our side. Nonetheless we will bring the Prophet of the Lord God, the President of the Church of Jesus Christ of Martian Saints to consider your words."

With that, he commanded all to ride away from the wagon. The scouts rode out about a mile to where the armies waited before Wilks commanded a halt.

"That thing has ears," he whispered darkly. "Sir Santos, I'm going to fetch the Prophet. You camp here and ensure that thing does not go far or do mischief. I fear a trap. These Earth demons are shrewd and not to be trusted. They speak of things we don't understand to confuse and frighten us. They call a woman president to mock the Priesthood. We will not be intimidated. I and my Adoni will travel swiftly to New Zion, but our beloved Prophet is old and will take many days to reach here. You remain until I return. In the meantime, it is time our armies understand the nature of the evil we fight."

🙿

The next several days were wondrous, Sir Santos and his commanders spent every moment they could talking with the Earthers. He had a feeling that if Wilks had thought about it, he would have forbidden the communication, but since he did not, they started a long conversation. It was awkward because of the time lapse between speaking and being spoken to. He learned that Earth was so far away that it took his words several minutes to fly there and theirs to return. It made the conversation stilted and slow, but of great worth. He was no fool, so did not talk of military matters nor did he give away their strength. But there was much to learn. And much he found strange.

He learned that cors were bred on Earth as well, but they were called unicorns. He was disappointed to learn that black cor were abundant on Earth and of no special achievement. He learned that there were striking differences between the people of South America and Greater Estonia. The first worshiped a strange invisible three-part god, and the latter worshiped no god at all. He was surprised to find that the Earthers had a sense of humor. They told him a few jokes that left him chuckling for days.

But he also learned some disturbing things. Between the planets was an expanse of airlessness where travel required mighty ships that carried their own air. He learned that the Earthers had vast stores of metal, and that steel was so abundant they could make buildings out of it. He learned they had created self-propelled vehicles and immense airships that could fly from one end of the planet to the other. He also learned that they hated and feared Mars, for Mars had done terrible things to their ancestors and put in place something that did not allow them out of their "atmosphere," which he took to mean something above their planet. He thought about the millions of steel balls.

There was much he did not understand about them and it was clear that they did not understand many of the things he said. They seemed especially interested in those called "computers," which seemed to be men of great learning who could handle complex tasks and had prodigious memories. He assured them that their computers were very good at what they did and that their memory was unsurpassed. They tried several times to get him to talk about military, but he would not be drawn out.

Sadly, one thing was absolutely clear: They had capabilities far beyond his own people's. The wagon itself was evidence of that, but more than that, they could talk of these remarkable feats such as flying between planets or flying across their planet in great "planes." These were people with powers found only in fairytales. Whenever they asked about how things were done on Mars, Sir Santos always answered cryptically, "Much like you do. Much like you do."

But it was clear to him that the people of Mars were nothing compared to these Earthers with their command of metal and air. At one point in the conversation, they had asked, "How do you power your cities?"

Carefully, he asked, "How do you power yours?"

They had answered, "Solar and nuclear mostly."

He had answered, "The same," but he did not know what they meant. He feared if he had said, "We do not power our cities, but rather power the people in them," they might have realized their advantage. What did it mean to power a city? A strange fear was growing in Sir Santos.

After fifteen days, the Prophet arrived. He came in a large black carriage trimmed in gold and silver. Thick red curtains were thrown back revealing his brightly smiling face. Cheers erupted from Sir Santos's army. Many of his army were from the outer reaches of lands around the Ort Sea; they did not often have the opportunity to see the Prophet in person. The carriage halted in the grass before the army and as the Prophet was helped down the steps placed there to assist him, the army broke into the hymn *Blessed, Holy, Prophet*

Dear. The transgens who had escorted the Prophet joined in. The President of the Church was clearly touched and, with water framing his eyes, he waved his bowler hat in the air and danced a jig.

"Sir Santos. It is good to see you. It may be that the Last Days are upon us. I will join you and Commander Wilks in your tent. I want to get your counsel before I talk with the so-called Earther's President."

The Prophet was clearly exhausted.

Sir Santos offered the aged man his elbow and escorted him toward his nearby tent. The Prophet's steps were slow but steady. He was two hundred fifty-seven years old and had been a prophet for nearly fifty. He was beloved by all and had had a long and productive reign. Sir Santos felt deep honor supporting this eminent man as they walked silently to his tent.

The Prophet bid he bring together his war council, and in a few minutes all seven of the war lords were assembled—along with Wilks.

"Brethren of the Priesthood, we gather here on the eve of war." The Prophet spoke with confidence. "The Earth demons will taste the resolve and determination of the Martian Church and I fear not that the Lord will stand at our side and bring us a swift and certain victory. There is no reason to fear and great reason to hope. May the Lord's blessings be upon you individually as you lead your army to war and upon you collectively in this great undertaking."

Lord Santos was somewhat confused by the Prophet's words. He could tell his war council was similarly confused. Many of them had been present during Sir Santos's conversations with the Earthers, and nothing had indicated that war was as inevitable as the Prophet seemed to suggest.

Commander Wilks joined in. "President, I will assure you that our forces will never be overcome. This war will end the Earth creatures' confidence in the arm of flesh."

Sir Santos slowly raised his arm to the square, seeking recognition. The Prophet nodded to him.

"My beloved Prophet. We rejoice in your presence here with us to day. I speak on behalf of all the men of these armies. We are your humble servants." There was some cheering by the commanders.

"My Lord, I assure you that, like your commander of the Adoni, we are ready to do battle with the Earthers—should it come to that. But Your Grace, I humbly submit that we who have remained here believe that the Earthers are here to sue for peace and want nothing more than to establish assurances that we have no intentions on their planet. I am convinced—"

Wilks jumped to his feet and shouted at the knight. "Are you a coward? Do we make peace with Satan? Do we deal with the Devil? You dare stand before the Prophet and suggest we compromise on truth and righteousness?"

The Prophet reached out and patted the leg of the fierce transgen. "Come, come, Commander. Let the man say his piece. I have come here to consider all counsel. Would you be surprised that sometimes even Elder Whitehead and I disagree?"

Wilks sat down almost sulkily and Sir Santos continued to lay his case before the Prophet. He told him about the conversations he had had with the Earthers, of the things he had learned about them: that they were likely children of Adam and not demons, and that they had power over metal.

When he confessed to having talked with the Earthers, Wilks looked as if he wanted slay the knight. Sir Santos openly expressed his concerns that they may have the technological advantage. Several of his war commanders chimed in and gave support to the things he was saying. A few he hoped would have said something did not, likely intimidated by the rage on the giant Adoni's face. But the Prophet listened attentively and when all had finished, he stood from his chair and spoke.

"I have heard interesting things this day. But it is clear to me that the Earthers are lying. Weak minds are easily influenced and deceived. Wilks has assured me of the intent of these devils, which our grandfathers so easily defeated, and I have received the sweet, still prompting within that tells me that Wilks knows whereof he speaks. My councilors and Elder Whitehead are in full agreement. I will speak to them by and by, but first I would like to speak to the armies to strengthen and embolden their courage for the battle ahead. Sir Santos, call the armies together."

Wilks helped him to his feet and supported him as he walked out of the tent and into the open air. Sir Santos called assembly, which was accomplished quickly and easily as most of the army was near the tent trying to get a glimpse of the Prophet. Sir Santos then set up a stage upon which the Prophet could stand, supported by Wilks who had not taken his eyes off him except to scowl at Sir Santos. The Prophet hobbled forward and with a trumpet held to his lips addressed the assembled army.

"Brethren of the Priesthood, we gather here on the eve of war. The Earth demons will taste the resolve and determination of the Martian Church and I fear not that the Lord will stand at our side and bring us a swift and certain victory. There is no reason to fear and great reason to hope. May the Lord's blessings be upon you individual captains as you lead your army to war, and upon you collectively in this great undertaking. In addition, I would like to add some instruction.

"All of you wear the blue feather in your helm as a symbol of the Church. It has become stylish in some of the outlining areas to wear this feather at a tilt. I have seen this trend spread throughout much of the land, and I find it disturbing to say the least, as do many of the Twelve Apostles. When I was a young warrior in the cavalry, we were always proud to wear our blue feather standing straight and tall upon our helms. We took great pride in ensuring that the blue feather symbolized what was in our hearts. We would no more put a tilt in the wearing of a blue feather than we would break one of the basic commandments. This tilt is not becoming of the way that servants of the Lord should wear their feathers, especially a feather representing the Church and Kingdom of the Living God. A tilt in the feather speaks of slackness and slovenliness. It speaks of weak-mindedness and debauchery. It is my hope that there will be no man found within the ranks of these great armies with the feather not standing up tall and straight. I hope that we will also teach our children to wear the blue feather standing, as it should be, with not a hint of a tilt. I think this is what the Apostle Paul was referring to when he said that 'to be carnally minded is death.' I encourage all of you to look to your feather and see that it is straight, true, and bright. May the Lord bless you in all your endeavors."

Wilks helped him off the stage to the wild cheering of the men, many of whom had removed their helms to straighten their feathers. The Prophet signaled Sir Santos over.

"Let us now go speak to the demons. And let me add, Sir Santos, that I have always admired the way you always wore your blue feather straight and true, just like your father did. Come. Let us see to these devils. I would like you and your seven to accompany me and Commander Wilks."

The Prophet continued to be supported by Wilks, but Sir Santos was deeply troubled. What had Wilks done to convince the Prophet that these Earthers were so nefarious? The transgen had only heard the woman from the other world once and knew nothing about the Earthers. Sir Santos had heard them many times and was convinced not only of their sincerity and desire for peace, but that they had vastly superior machines, which likely implied vastly superior weapons.

They arrived at the wagon. Without ceremony, Wilks shouted at it, "Earthers. I bring before you the Prophet of the Living God. The President of the Church of Jesus Christ of Martian Saints. The High Priest of Mars. His Grace, President Sanders."

The Prophet was about to speak, but Sir Santos spoke quickly, "Your Grace, the voices travel slowly across the void between Earth and Mars. It will take a few minutes to receive a reply."

The Prophet nodded and Wilks scowled menacingly at the knight. After a time the wagon came alive.

Welcome President Sanders. It is an honor for me to speak to you across the miles between our planets. As I said to your able commanders, we seek to establish a peaceful relationship between our worlds. For too long we have been separated by an immense distance, and for too long have held unnecessary fears and suspicions. We believe that we have much to offer your people. We have made great advances in medicine, philosophy, genetic engineering, nanotechnology, literature, and computer technology. Now at last we offer you our hand across the vastness of space. We have seen from afar your fair fields, and the breathtaking way your terraforming efforts have unfolded into a beautiful and ecologically stable world. However, we have been through a great period of darkness and war due to our last conflict with your planet. Only in the last hundred years have our abilities reached that of our ancestors. We are unsure of what brought about that terrible and ruinous war between our worlds, but we know that we are one people and we humbly extend our hand in friendship and fellowship. We would like to discuss ways to remove the blockade placed in our upper atmosphere. We would like to resume trade. I, President Borges, hope that you will join me in forging a strong alliance of mutual benefit and lasting peace.

Sir Santos could not help but mark the distasteful scowl that had set upon the Prophet's face the moment the message began coming through. The beloved man fidgeted and kept glancing up at Wilks, whose stern face was a mask of disgust. When the message stopped, Wilks whispered to the Prophet's ear. The Prophet nodded repeatedly and then looked at Wilks and patted his cheek affectionately. He then turned to Sir Santos and asked, "How do I speak to them?"

Sir Santos thought he might have just a moment. "You just begin speaking in a normal tone of voice, my Lord, but before you begin, may I respectfully offer my opinion that these Earthers are sincere . . ."

"Silence, dog!" Wilks spat at him in a harsh whisper, then turned earnestly to the Prophet. "My Grace, he has done enough damage. Now is not the time to listen to Satan's lies."

The Prophet turned to Sir Santos and placed his finger over his pursed lips signaling silence. He then smoothed his suit and cleared his throat.

"Earthers, you speak whereof you do not understand. We come here on the eve of war. You will taste the resolve and determination of the Church and I fear not that the Lord will stand at our side and bring us a swift and certain victory. There is great reason for you to fear and great reason for us to hope. May the Lord's blessings be upon us in this great undertaking, for you will find yourself again smitten in such a manner that you will not rise from the dust for another many hundreds of years. By the power of the Priesthood you will be smitten. Send your flying war cor. We will cut them down. We do not fear you. Know you not that we have over a thousand Adoni standing ready to smite you bone and marrow? Do you think you can stand against us? The prophets of old warned you. You were never to contact us again. You have awakened the sleeping boxes to which we have listened since your defeat; we listened to ensure your compliance. And now, against all warnings, you have started your Satanic chatter once again.

"Then, in an affront to all the dignity of Mars, you send this abomination, this ungodly wagon from your demon-filled Earth. You will feel the wrath of the Lord as proclaimed by His servants. We will cut you off, root and branch. As the Lord said unto Joshua as they entered the Promised Land, we will destroy you: man, woman, and child. I am the President of the Church of Jesus Christ of Martian Saints and you will be cut down like the Gadianton Robbers of old."

Sir Santos was horrified. He did not know what to do. He looked at his commanders and saw only confusion written on their faces. Was it to be war then? Against what kind of enemy? No one spoke as they waited for a reply. When it came it sent chills through the knight and his commanders:

So be it.

That night a feast was held for the Prophet. Several wagon masters had arrived with the Prophet's carriage and his personal staff.

In swift order they conjured abundant courses of dodo, water buffalo, maize cakes, watercress, pickled beets, salmon, Ort Sea perch, turkey and duck eggs pickled in white wine vinegar, rice casserole, seven cheeses, and green pony-hoof gelatin with carrots.

Sir Santos was in no mood for the festivities. He walked alone into the grasslands. A soft breeze was blowing off the sea and Earth was just starting to set. How could such a beautiful star harbor such nemeses? Or did it? Was it his people or (dare he think it?) their prophet who was the monster? He found himself meandering down to the Earth wagon where it had not moved for the weeks they had camped there. He walked up and sat down before it looking at the red blinking light shining even more brightly in the darkness. Had the Father in Heaven really told the Prophet to start a conflict with these people? Surely the God's mouthpiece here on Mars was above reproach, or so he had always believed. Yet now the Prophet's actions had not only seemed unwise, they seemed misdirected. He was asking them to risk their existence on his insistence that the Earthers could be defeated by a handful of arrogant transgen giants.

He looked at the Earth wagon. The subtlety by which it had been crafted was far beyond anything that could be done on this planet. He knelt where he was and tried to pray but he could not find the words, or was it the humility he lacked? Why not trust the Prophet? That was what he had spent his life teaching his children. That was why he had fought three wars with heretics. But now? Something seemed wrong.

Sir Santos. It is good to see you tonight.

Sir Santos jumped at the voice, but quickly settled down as he recognized the familiar voice of his distant friend the President of the southern continent.

"Hello, President Borges. Things did not go well, did they?"

The long pauses between replies left him more and more convinced that war with a people that could traverse such distances with a self-propelled wagon was a fool's quest. Tonight their conversation seemed awkward and unanimated. Times had indeed changed. By the time the short and stilted conversation was over, the knight had learned some things that frightened him, but also gave him a new resolve.

"President. Give me a month or so. I am determined not to let this come to war. Will you give me that? I will convince the Prophet that this is not in our or your interest. Will you grant me a month?"

The reply in its time came.

Of course. But we will be watching the skies. If you launch an attack we will be ready.

When Sir Santos returned to his tent, he told his servant to contact the seven commanders and meet him on the hillock north of the camp. As he found his mount, he stroked the sides of his magnificent black war cor. The feasting had ended and the tent of the Prophet was dark and silent. In the distance, he could hear the singing of the transgens camped on the flat to the north. Their hymn might have once provoked a feeling of reverence, as they voiced the sacred hymns of his youth, but now it seemed a hollow foreboding that portended ignorance and poverty of thought.

The seven commanders came as commanded. No one spoke as they gathered and their mood was black. For a moment Sir Santos thought it might have been the lateness of the hour, but he soon learned that none of them had been sleeping.

Sir Santos began. "It seems that our beloved Prophet has chosen war, and my sense is that it will soon be upon us. We have much to do to ready. I do not share His Grace's optimism that the transgens will make a difference. I need your thoughts and I need them honestly. What is our course of action? Sir Ita? What was meant by your grunt?"

Sir Ita set his jaw, but turned away. "I meant nothing."

Sir Santos considered him a moment. "You meant something. You meant what I think all of us are thinking. Is any man here anxious to fight this war with the Earthers?"

Sir Ita spoke up, slowly at first, but picking up heat as he spoke. "I am old and have been in many battles. I know war like I know my own household. But how do we fight an enemy whose strength we cannot know? We don't even know what weapons they use, but I suspect they may be terrible. The headmaster at the school at New Moab told me that the crater that is now Lake Kimball was made by a house-size piece of rock that fell from the sky. If these Earthers can toss things from the sky, as we know they can, as we can see from the wagon they sent, we may not even see them coming as they toss things upon our cities at their leisure. In the end we will be wasted without even bloodying a sword."

There were nods of assent. Another added, "We don't know their numbers. We don't know their weapons. And lastly we cannot bring the war to their world. It must be fought here."

Sir Tembean seemed to be talking to himself as he spoke, "The fabric they sent with the wagon from the sky. I've never seen its like. It is stronger than canvas, yet lighter than the strand of spider web. It is not made of flax, hemp, cotton, or wool. If they can make such use of fabric, what else can they do?"

Sir Tong frowned. "But the Lord knows what they can do. And if he told the Prophet to fight, then we will prosper in the end. Many times a campaign that seems doomed can succeed if we rely on the strength of the Lord. Remember when Nephi's brothers Laman and Lemuel complained that the Lord could not deliver Laban into their hands because he was a mighty man and could command fifty?" Sir Tong then looked into the sky, "As the scripture says, 'Let us go up again into Jerusalem, and let us be faithful in keeping the commandments of the Lord; for behold he is mightier than all the earth, then why not mightier than Laban and his fifty, yea, or even than his tens of thousands?' Should our faith be any less?"

There were nods of agreement, but Sir Alma spoke. "Something is wrong here. The Prophet spoke to us about our feather today. Do you believe that the Lord cares how we wear our feather on the verge of perhaps the greatest war we have ever fought? Besides, his faith in these transgens is misplaced. They are mighty. But they are few, and again what is to say that the Earthers don't have transgens?"

Sir Santos bowed his head. "The Earthers *are* transgens."

Those gathered looked up in surprise. "I teased from President Borges something about themselves. They have had many years of darkness, but during that time they bred freely with transgens, or as they call them transgenic humans. But her description was clear."

Sir Santos rubbed his face with his hand. "As all you know I have bred cor for many year seeking the best characteristics. I suspect that the breeding stock of our own Martian transgens has been of limited stock, as it were. To breed the finest cor I travel the world, bringing together the best stock to create the features I wanted. These transgen, while mighty, seem lacking in some ways. They seem too focused, too limited in expression—quite humorless and quick to anger. They seem inbred, if you'll forgive me for saying so, and made to follow orders, not give them. This is not true of the Earthers. They are curious, articulate, and have a wry sense of humor. If it is to be war, then it will be against humans that might have the strength and quickness of the transgens, and our own level of intelligence."

Sir Santos took a breath, "But there's more."

The gathered knights stared silently, waiting.

"The Church, Joseph's original, The Church of Jesus Christ of Latter-day Saints, exists on the Earth."

"What!" Sir Ita staggered back.

"It's true. President Borges said it was one of the larger churches on Earth."

"But that can't be," Sir Tong said, "That would imply there are two prophets. Impossible."

"It is what she said."

There was a long silence, until Sir Tong said, "I move that we take these concerns to the Prophet. Surely he will listen to reason about this new information and if this is from the Lord then he can tell us how the revelation came and why our lives and those of our families should be placed at such risk. And what we should do if we risk fighting brethren in the gospel!"

The next morning after breakfast the Prophet agreed to see Sir Santos. It took some effort to see him alone, and Wilks was angry with Sir Santos's insistence that he visit with His Grace alone.

Once alone with the Prophet, he laid out the concerns raised the other night. He explained that there might be lost brethren on Earth. The Prophet listened attentively, even asking some clarifying questions, but in the end he shook his white-haired head.

"Sir Santos. Who am I?"

"You are the President of the Church of Jesus Christ of Martian Saints. You are the Prophet."

"And yet you doubt me?"

"No my Lord, I just have concerns."

"And who are you to have concerns?"

"I am a Knight of the Kingdom. I am one of your generals."

"No." The aged man paused then continued, "No. No longer. I cannot have you leading men when you will not be led yourself. I do not need to justify my revelations to you. The Lord speaks through me. That the demons claim to have the true church is a lie—a cheap tactic to trick weaker spirits. I saw in my mind the arrival of their armies arrayed for battle riding on great white flying war cor. I saw them come in a dream, and I saw them face our armies. The Earthers were dead within a day. So I saw. So it will be. Go sit in your house while we fight the Earthers."

"But Your Grace. They don't have flying war cor. I asked. They will come in great flying wagons . . ."

"You may go. Send in Wilks and get me Sir Ita. He will lead my armies under Commander Wilks. I will not have a doubter lead my armies to glory and honor in our war with the Earth demons."

Wilks was waiting by the door. There was little doubt he had been listening. He smirked as Sir Santos passed, but Sir Santos did not even look up at him.

Sir Santos walked slowly back to his tent. The morning sun was just burning the haze from the grass and the smell of the alfalfa flowers was strong on the breeze. He met Sir Ita on the way and told him what the Prophet had said.

"Sir Santos. Hold. We will meet again tonight." Ita looked troubled.

Sir Santos nodded.

Later that night, Sir Santos laid out his talk with the Prophet. Even Sir Tong seemed disturbed by the news. Sir Santos was well loved and known as a warrior of excellence. To be stripped of rank and told to go home was not only an insult, it was unprecedented and strange. There was a long silence. Suddenly Sir Ita stepped forward and upon one knee offered his sword.

"Sir Santos. I will be led by you."

Sir Santos stepped back. "You speak heresy."

"Yes. I fear it is. But for a long time perhaps the heretics have seen something that I have been slow to see. We went to war with Sir Kendell when he dissented from the Church because the Church had taken his lands for their own pasture. We went to war with Sir Kim because the Church demanded that we wear only the shifts made by the Church workhouses in New Zion, when, for as long as we have memory, the shifts were made in New Moab by Sir Talon's people from the wool grown of sheep raised on the slopes of Olympus Mons. But the Church needed money for its coffers, and took over those folks' livelihood. In each case, was there any one of us that thought the Church's cause was just? We went for loyalty's sake. Blind obedience was the only reason we can give for our actions, but the actions of the Church were wrong! No more. I am a heretic."

The silence that followed this declaration was stunning.

Suddenly at his side was his son, Sir Alma. "I too will stand by your side."

"Knights! How can you do this thing? Have we not all sworn fealty to the Prophet? Do we not owe him our lives?" Sir Santos said quietly to the kneeling men.

"What of our obligations to our wives? To our children? To those we hold stewardship over? What weight does our fealty carry to the Prophet when these things are added to the scales? We have sat in council with the Prophet. He is a man as we are. He has claimed no vision from heaven. No angel has appeared. As far as I can tell his words are coming from what you have called an inbred transgen!" So saying, Sir Ita pushed the hilt of his sword toward Sir Santos.

Suddenly Sir Tong arose. All eyes in the tent turned to him. He was quick to defend any offense made to the leaders of the Church. He stood and surveyed the men assembled and slowly began to speak:

"My fellow knights. You know me. You know my heart. What you now propose goes against all that I have believed, all I have fought for, and all I have stood for since my baptism at age eight by the hand of my father. If the Prophet were to ask me to fall upon my sword, I would do so without hesitation . . . or so I would have. But I have sat with Sir Santos by the wagon for many hours and am convinced that if we go to war with Earth, we will all die with our families. But death is not my concern. Should the good Lord wish to send us all to his Kingdom at this time, I would gladly go there. But I will not go there under a man's best guess.

"My obligation is not to the Prophet, but to Him that he represents. In this matter, I feel nothing in my heart that bids me follow him into this madness. If the Spirit whispered that I should follow him in this war, I would follow the Prophet into the depths of insanity. In this, however, I am convinced he speaks as a man.

"Alas, these are not the days of Joseph, Brigham, Hinckley, or Nather and it as been long indeed since our prophets claimed to speak directly to the physical Lord. Opinion seems to rule over revelation and to the extent that he does give his opinion he is open to a man's frailties and errors. It is our individual obligation to seek a higher confirmation that the Prophet speaks as such. In this, I believe he does not.

"Sir Santos, in this I, too, am your man. But be warned. Should you use this opportunity to enter into open war with the Church or its leaders I will be the first to cut you down. But in stopping this war with Earth, I am with you. I am your servant."

One by one, they were joined by the others until at last even the aged Sir Baglet knelt at his side holding his sword out to him as the others had now done. And one by one he laid his hand upon their hilt and head and raised them up.

He stood before them and scratched his beard, deep in thought. Venus was just rising and the night would soon be over.

"Our action must stay in this circle. Many of our men would not understand our reasons, nor should they need to. Our dissent from the Church's head must be subtle. Like the scriptures say, we must be 'as wise as serpents' and as 'harmless as doves.'" He looked out over his captains and gave a sorrowful sigh. "Sir Alma. How many men wait for you at Dimple Downs, and have they seen the transgens?"

"They have not seen the transgens, nor heard any word of them. I have about twelve thousand in my cavalry and twenty thousand footmen."

"As I thought. I give to you the greatest challenge then. Ride to the transgen citadel in the Phlegras and sack the city. Tell your captains that the Earthers have established a city there. Do not underestimate their abilities. They will have nearly a thousand men left there and you face a long and bloody battle. Even worse, women and children may fight, but spare them as you can."

"And if they surrender?"

"Honor them if they do, but do not expect it. They have been trained from their youth to seek a glorious death in battle. We have here about nine hundred war cor and a thousand spearmen. How many archers?"

"Less than seven score, my Lord," Sir Ita answered.

"It will have to do. Are the transgens still singing?"

"Yes," said Sir Tong. They all knew what his next command would be.

"Sir Ita. Lead your men against the transgens here. Start by using the archers and be quick. The armies must believe that they are in league with the Earthers."

Sir Santos suddenly bit his lower lip. "What have we become if we kill mercilessly those we have no quarrel with?"

Sir Ita put his arm around him, "Truth and war do not go well together. What is the alternative? This war cannot come to pass. It simply cannot."

Sir Tong added, "And as the angel said to Nephi, 'It is better that one man should perish than a whole nation perish in unbelief.' Better the transgens now here. The Prophet is under their influence. What can we do?"

Sir Santos nodded. "Then it is better to put the transgens to the sword than let our planet pass away."

"What of the Prophet?" Sir Baglet looked deeply troubled.

"I will take care of the Prophet," said Sir Santos firmly. "Not a hair of his head will be harmed, brethren. That, I promise you. He may be misguided, but he is still the Prophet."

Sir Santos was near tears. "Gather your army swiftly and silently. When you see the lamp in the Prophet's tent alight, attack."

"Your Grace, the Earth demons have attacked!"

Sir Santos burst into the Prophet's tent holding aloft his lantern. His transgen guards jumped to their feet, their steel swords drawn and ready.

"Wilks asks for you! I will guard the Prophet. Go!"

The Prophet, too, had leapt up surprisingly swiftly. The Church president nodded to the two guards, who rushed to join the sudden sound of battle.

"Where?"

"On the plain below."

The Prophet rushed to the door, but Sir Santos intercepted him. "No, Your Grace. The Earth monsters are searching for you high and low. You must not let your face be shown. Let me be your eyes and ears."

"Yes. Yes you are right of course. But why are not you in the battle?"

"You have relieved me, Your Grace. Remember?"

"Oh, yes. Well then, what is happening?"

Sir Santos moved to the door and peered out. "President Sanders, it is a terrible battle! Great white flying war cor are descending from the sky."

"I knew it!"

"They are landing upon the ground, but the Adoni are upon them. They are fighting like the very angels of heaven."

The sounds of battle permeated the tent. The screams of men and cor rent the air. Steel on steel. Steel on flesh. The twang of arrows being sent into flight and the sickening thud when they found their mark.

"What's happening?" the Prophet yelled impatiently as Sir Santos had gone silent. The battle below him was like nothing he had ever seen. The transgens *were* fighting like dragons. Their swords sang in the air as if animated by a fire of their own. For every one of the Adoni slain, fifteen of Sir Santos's force lay torn asunder by the wrath of these ill-bred demons. Great war cor lay scattered about the battlefield, with wounded and dead men flung all around.

"Sir Santos, what is happening?"

Sir Santos looked at the Prophet, afraid the old man could see the fear etched on his own face. "The Adoni are fighting like nothing I've seen. Their speed is like that of a popmaize kernel exploding."

The Prophet laughed. "Are they winning?"

"Yes."

But what the transgens had in strength, they lacked in numbers. While a transgen is engaged with four of Sir Santos's men, a spearman would slip behind and thrust a spear deep into his spine, cutting off his legs and allowing the others to slip in and kill him. One by one, the transgens were dying. The tide had turned, but at what cost?

"What devilry is this?" Lord Santos said, as if to himself.

"What is it?" The Prophet said breathlessly.

"Whenever an Earther or its flying cor dies the others cast a powder upon it and it disappears," Sir Santos said.

"No! They are sorcerers as well!" cried the Prophet.

"So it would seem."

"The devils!" The Prophet scowled.

"They are focusing on the Adoni. They recognize their strength. Sir, the slaughter is great."

The battle seemed to go on for hours, but in reality it was less than one. The transgen were slain, but the battle was terrible. So many had been killed. Sir Santos sobbed as the Prophet put his arm around him.

"It was as I foresaw. The Earthers have been defeated. Who could stand against my army of Adoni?"

"Yes, Your Grace. Who could stand?"

The Prophet bowed in sorrow. "They slew them all? How is that possible?"

Sir Santos looked deep into the Prophet's eyes and found emptiness.

"A great loss" was all that Sir Santos could muster.

They walked through the field of the dead. The Prophet seemed worn and fragile and took no notice of the Martian regulars that lay scattered about the field in droves. He commented occasionally at the loss of a cor, but of the others he said nothing. Only his precious Adoni currently occupied his grief.

After the battle, Sir Santos had contacted Sir Tembean who had an army of 13,000 waiting a less than 150 kilometers away and sent them to join Sir Alma in their conquest of Adoniha. They were going to need every man. He also sent with them Sir Ita who had been in the battle with the transgens in order to prepare the army heading for Adoniha for the kind of fighting that would be necessary for the battle. Archery and spears were what turned the battle against the transgens. The importance of these units could not be overestimated in the coming battle; in close hand-to-hand combat, the transgens were indomitable.

"The Earth demons will pay for this," the Prophet said quietly. "The fact that the ordinary men were able to drive them off after the dogs had been nearly destroyed by the Adoni says to me that we will prevail. They will face the Adoni again and in greater numbers next time. We will see how brave they are then."

Sir Santos did not say anything. Heaviness weighed upon him despite the victory of his armies. He was convinced he had saved his beloved planet, yet at the cost of betraying everything he had ever believed.

"Sir Santos," the Prophet said kindly, "in the meantime, I feel impressed by the Holy Spirit to reinstate you as the commander of my armies. You have been a strength to me in this and I will reward it. With Wilks dead—" And here his voice choked. "—I will need strong leadership until another Adoni commander can be chosen." The Prophet suddenly began to sob. "We will build a temple in this spot to commemorate the death of these mighty men. So terrible a loss. So terrible a loss."

Sir Santos knelt, as he was expected to, and pointed the hilt of his sword toward the Prophet. The holy man placed his hands upon the hilt and Sir Santos's head and lifted him to his feet.

"I, for one, am glad you are here," the Prophet said, smiling sadly at Sir Santos.

"I am glad, also," the knight responded, casting his eyes toward the ground.

It was nearly two weeks before the news came. Sir Santos was impressed that the Prophet had stayed at the battle site and personally dedicated the grave of every man slain, both the regular brethren and the Adoni. The action seemed strange to many in the army who had been told that the Adoni had been in league with the Earthers, but Sir Santos's commanders portrayed it as an example of Christlike forgiveness—an act of unrestrained mercy.

The rider reported to Sir Santos first, who nodded sadly when told that while the Adoni had been slain, it had been at the cost the lives of nearly ten thousand men. The report of the battle sent shivers of sorrow through the knight as he listened.

Because Sir Santos's armies carried the Prophet's banner, they had been welcomed into the city. Were it not for that, there is little doubt the city could have maintained a siege indefinitely. The fighting had been monstrous. Both the male and female transgens had fought tirelessly. It was again only by dint of sheer numbers that Sir Santos's army had prevailed. The transgens had never given up. Surrender would not be accepted, even when only ten of them remained alive and the battle was all but over. Sadly, even children had joined the battle and the only transgens to remain alive were a few of the babies and very young children. Even many of those had died at the hands of battle-maddened soldiers drunk with blood, believing they were Earth demons who deserved to die.

Sir Santos found the Prophet in his tent. The old man was in a somber mood, having come from dedicating the last of the graves of the men in battle.

"Your Grace. I fear I bring sorrow upon sorrow. The Earthers have attacked the city of Adoniha. None have survived."

The Prophet staggered back. "It cannot be! Who said this? It is a lie. The city is full of our finest Adoni. They are invincible. The Lord has whispered to me that they would prevail. This can't . . . This is . . . This . . ." Suddenly the Prophet fell forward, his eyes rolling back into his head as a seizure rippled through his aged body. Sir Santos carried him respectfully to his bed, laid him down, and covered his shaking body with a warm wool blanket.

The knight called for the Prophet's medical attendants who quickly rushed to his side and began to wipe his sweating brow. They frantically tried to administer healing spirits from their colored bottles, but Sir Santos had little hope in their skill. Whose heart could survive such loss?

Sir Santos staggered out of the tent and vomited violently. The deed was done. The betrayal complete. He staggered to his own tent and lay upon his bed and stared coldly at the ceiling. A numbness seemed to spread over his soul. The depth of his betrayal seemed to choke his emotions. He lay stunned. *What have I done? What have I done? What have I done?*

The wagon clicked at last and the voice returned.

While we are saddened at your reluctance to come to know us better, we will agree that for one hundred years we will have a silence of peace between our people. As you said, this will give our people time to adjust to the idea of our contact and perhaps learn to forget old hatreds and long-standing disagreements. We thank Sir Santos for negotiating this peace and congratulate him on his call to the apostolic office. And most heartily we thank you, President Whitehead, for agreeing to these accords. We hope that in the intervening time we may teach our children to not think of each other as enemies, but rather long-separated brothers and sisters. With this communication we bid you adieu.

The new Prophet President Whitehead sighed as Sir Santos helped him to his feet. They walked away as the remaining guard covered the wagon with sticks and prepared to immolate it as agreed in the treaty that Sir Santos had negotiated.

"One hundred years," the Prophet sighed.

"Yes," Sir Santos said quietly.

"We must spend that time in preparing for their contact. We have only a handful of Adoni, mostly children, who remain after the attack. We must start a breeding program as soon as possible, as President Sanders had planned."

"With respect, President, as the newest member of the Council of the Twelve Apostles and as your new first counselor, I think we must first learn how to fly."

The two men continued in conversation as they walked over the windblown prairie toward the carriages that had brought them here. One man was God's new spokesman for an entire planet; the other, a man who believed himself damned, but who loved Mars more than his own soul.

Rennact

I HATE FIFTH SUNDAYS. ESPECIALLY WHEN I'M IN charge. The Rennact went well, despite Bro. Tellic being an emotional mess. This is his third pregnancy and you would think he would be used to it, but I found him weeping in the baptismal font like a silly baby. He was curled up on the tiles watching bcasts to his visual cortex of his last birth. I talked him into joining us and finally he did, but I wish his wife would keep a better eye on him. We all know what he's like when he forgets his Natalex®.

Getting the children into position after the two-hour block is nearly impossible. We lined up on the Willy on the north side of the chapel. The children are so adorable. Sis. Wendle had programmed the bcast of a cold Wyoming winter and when I checked into what the children were seeing it was very well done, but about half the children were off-channel going to places like Blandals Snoobles, or that new one, Titan's Wacky Revenge (which my kids can't seem to stay away from). After seizing their input streams we finally got them back under control and lined up for the procession on the Willy. Bro. and Sis. Candle have done a wonderful job cleaning the path of debris so that we don't trip. I'm still a little chagrinned about how shabby our Willy has become. I saw a chapel in Rio that had a Willy nearly fifty feet wide and surfaced like an Olympic 400m track. I guess that Arkansas will have to grow more before we get the good stuff.

It's always one thing or another. I asked Sis. Smith to lead us around the Willy so she got to pick the song and at least that was ready to go on time, but Old Widow Thissle (who really doesn't look her fifteen decades) started a harangue about how in her day the Martins were actually pulled by hand and attached by a rope not bcast-controlled plastic automatons. As can be imagined, the children were quickly bored and I could detect some of the kids switching channels because she was going on and on (it's amazing how some parents have such poor control over their kids' streams!). The trouble worsened when Sis. Wendle's Wyoming blizzard got so bad that Sis. Thissle's words were drowned by the sound of the wind. When she finally finished, we were standing in a foot of virtual snow!

When she finally concluded, we downspun the bcast and came back to reality for the judging of the Martins. Bishop Kim—in full pioneer regalia—was in rare form! He acted and maneuvered just like a real person from the 19th Century; very funny. I love when he judges the Martins rather than his councilors. No offense to them, but he really sparkles the plasma red and gold. Some of the kids had done some flatel work! Carlos Moretta's family, very traditional, had stuck to the guidelines brilliantly. They had put together a classic wagon with a team of four oxen harnessed and pulling. The oxen were 3D Printformed in reddish brown plastic, and as they walked forward, lowing and swaying their great heads, I almost felt I was seeing what the pioneers saw. Bravo, Morettas, for setting the tone for the Fifth Sunday Rennact!

Others were not so "traditionally rendered." There were some sleighs pulled by reindeer and such, but the worst was little Jim Cahill who I swear receives no supervision at all. He had the Pluto International Rover being pulled by a dragon. It was nearly a sixth of a meter long, with a quarter meter wingspan. The PIR was another sixth of a meter, but that's not the bad part. The worst thing was when the dragon attacked little Missy Jang's Rainbow Unicorns pulling a "Little Red Wagon." Sure enough, a quick look at the drag-on's instruction set by Bishop Kim and it was clear the beast was programmed for combat. It was thrown into the recbin. I must say Jimmy looked repentant, but his parents just shrugged it off like it was a cute wimstickle. You can see why he acts the way he does. The ward clerk ran into the office and Printformed another of Missy's Unicorns and wagon, but still.

The Bishop picked, of course, the Carlos wagon and team to lead the Martins around the Willy. Sis. Littleton then performed the recitation.

Westle Prim sifted wheat flour over the Martins as Sis. Littleton said,

"We brought wheat that we may not be hungry."

Then Bro. Tellic said,

"We brought whale oil to light our way."

And Missy Jang poured the genetically manufactured humpback oil over the Martins.

Sis. Littleton, again,

"We brought scriptures to open the heavens."

And Doghin Kimball scattered the confetti made from old print scriptures over the Martins.

Then everyone said together,

"We brought our Faith to share with the world!"

Then we all bcast up to the Wyoming winter and started walking through the virtual blizzard, our Martins, now rendered digitally in the simulation, striding beside us. The Willy-actual rendered in the bcast was a blue ghost stripe that showed the path. I wondered what the pioneers would have made of this procession. The classic oxen was one Martin they would surely recognize, but the unicorns, dolphins, apes, Doberman pincers, bears, and wasps, pulling covered wagons, sleighs, space shuttles and doughnuts would have been a strange sight indeed. My husband said that the procession around the Willy from outside the bcast looked very solemn and dignified and he thought it was well done. He especially liked the bears pulling a pumpkin carriage. The little rendered plastik bears would stop every few feet and bow, eyes closed, as if praying.

But I worry. The Fifth Sunday Rennact is just not my cup of tea. I know. I know. It is a sacred tradition within the church and I ought to do it with a better attitude. Watching the little kids and their excitement rounding the Willy was almost enough to help me remember why we do things like this, but it was really the old Primary song that finally got to me.

When we came to the Rock of Remembrance, we opened our digital song books, and sang the old pioneer ditty, "Stairway to Heaven."* When we reach the chorus about everything being one, and about being a rock and not rolling, I feel myself choking up. And suddenly I found tears in my eyes and the spirit and promise of those old pioneers who lived so long ago seemed to come upon me and I remembered why we do these Fifth Sunday Rennacts.

---

*"Stairway to Heaven." Robert Plant and Jimmy Page, *Children's Hymns and Songs,* 2112. LDS.

A Strange Report from the Church Archives

NOTES FOR MY REPORT ON POSSIBILITY MACHINES BY *Elder James Talmage, Salt Lake City Apostle of the Church of Jesus Christ of Latter-day Saints August 4, 1916*

Dear President Joseph F. Smith and Elders Lund and Smith:

I thank your secretary for providing me with this quire. Herein I will record the notes for my report on the "Possibility Machines" that you asked me to investigate under the authority of the First Presidency. Pursuant to the facts, I believe that the people of Washington County indeed have been engaged in procuring certain objects from a cunning conman by the name Willard Bayes. I will endeavor to be as thorough as possible while avoiding the palaver of those we interview for this account. It appears that Mr. Bayes is a rather accomplished mesmerer and as such has provoked the minds of those with whom he dealt to wonderful imaginings filled with meretricious ideas relating to his person and abilities. My hope is that given my training in science, I will be immune to such manipulations. But we will see, for it appears that hale men of sound mind have also been taken in.

27 June 1916
I travelled with Elders Richards and Whitney down to St. George. As we arrived, the remnants of a storm were departing to the North

and the sun was starting to shine, although the day was cooler than normal and clouds in the Southeast were yet menacing. Pres. Dole welcomed us to his house; his wife set before us a delicious lunch of biscuits and brown gravy with a fresh hot sage tea which warmed our hearts and spirits. However, when we got down to business, the mention of Mr. Bayes produced a visible pall on the faces of both President and Sis. Dole. A shadow seemed to be cast over Pres. Dole's visage, and Sis. Dole departed the room in some manifest haste and did not return to clear away our plates or serve a promised apple pie.

He admitted that he had indeed had dealings with Mr. Bayes, but argued that he was a harmless carnival man and that his claims and curious devices were nothing but innocuous amusements such as might be had in any parlor in Salt Lake City. He seemed defensive, and we ascertained that he was directing us away from the matter at hand. We insisted under the authority of the priesthood that the items he had procured from the man be brought forth. Still, he hesitated, and after some dissembling and much running his fingers through his thin grey hair he arose and went into the back bedrooms where we could hear a muted and indistinct but heated discussion with his wife.

At last he emerged and insouciantly tossed into my hands a simple windup toy such as might be had from any five and dime. It was smaller than those with which I'm familiar, but in design there was nothing that was not typical of such devices. It was a small red-breasted bird, handed-painted, and cast of tin. I gave the shiny key on its back a couple of turns and placed it on the ground where it carelessly hopped about clacking and clicking after the manner of such things. It brought a smile to my face and I thought how delighted my daughter would be at such a trick. But the look on Pres. Dole's face was one of abject horror and fear. Had I seen only his face, and not that which brought about his fright, I might have thought Death's scythe was being swung my direction in full vigor. Upon seeing my countenance toward him, he recovered admirably and watched without expression as the machine wound down to stillness.

I was about to remark on the thing, when he held up his hand in such a way as to silence me. He then picked up the toy and quickly carried it from the room. I could not be sure, but it seemed that I heard a quiet weeping from his wife as he returned. He sat down and asked what I thought of the windup bird. I told him that it seemed harmless enough and hardly worth the attention of the brethren in Salt Lake. He nodded and then asked rather abruptly what I missed most since coming from England. I did not hesitate and told him what I wished for most was a good cup of English tea. I know many of the brethren frowned on such indulgences, but I found no harm in an occasional cup. At that moment there was a knock at the door. It was Brother and Sister Sally's boy (who you'll remember from our previous visit made a wondrously fine drawing of the St. George Temple) with a parcel that had come on the train from Phoenix. It was a package of nothing less than a half-stone of Brooke Bond Builder's tea, something I had not thought to see again in this life. The coincidence was striking and gave us a good laugh, which continued as Sis. Dole put a kettle to boil. I asked how it was that he had thought to order such an extravagant item and he walked over to a desk and pulled from one of the cubbies a signed order for the tea at the cost of nearly $50. He said he remembered very well ordering the tea, although he could not account for his reasons for the order.

He explained that the windup he had bought from Mr. Bayes was claimed to have certain powers over time itself. He had been told that it had three uses. When they got home that night, they wound the little creature up and watched it dance. They wished that their son were home from his mission in the isles of the Pacific.

The second we had uttered the wish we thought what a foolish one it had been, for on the mantle was a well-read telegram announcing his arrival to San Francisco from the Islands and the promise that he would be home that very day on the 5:15. We had prepared his room for arrival and he was scheduled to talk at stake conference two Sunday's hence. With all these preparations in place, why had we wished for what was inevitable and already going to happen? He scratched his head and looked me in the eye and said slowly, *What I wonder is if it was as inevitable as it seemed before I uttered the wish. I am deeply troubled.*

Being of scientific sensibilities, I asked that the device be brought back and that we give it another test. But his wife utterly refused us, saying we had wasted one of their "realignments" as she called it, and that, *Each family can only buy one and that cost us a pretty penny, not to mention the $50 we are out for your tea!* She was quite angry and we acceded to her request.

We visited several families who had bought the devices. Not all were birds. There were frogs, bears, Indians with moving tomahawks, and such. But all of the Saints we interviewed claimed strange stories. The most troubling was the Westfields's. They had brought home a little jumping mouse windup and on their first night wished for something that set the hair on the back of my neck standing up. They said that when they came home from buying a device from Mr. Bayes, there was only one thing they had wished for all their lives. *We wished that our dear baby son had never died sixteen years ago. I don't know why we would ask for such a thing, for there he was sitting on the divan just like always, looking at us as if we were quite mad. He had come in from feeding the pigs and had just changed his attire to attend a game of charades at the Varner's house with some of his schoolmates.*

Among those harboring the devices, such stories were common, although none so dramatic. The sheer multitude of stories was concerning. One could have ascribed them to a mass mesmerizing by a clever charlatan, for such things are certainly known to occur. However, we were unsettled in our minds, and after a thoughtful prayer decided to visit Mr. Bayes ourselves and investigate the matter more fully. Elder Richards, with full apostolic authority, warned those who had machines not to use them until we returned with our report to the First Presidency, for we suspected that if they did work in some manner, it was by darker powers than the Saints had before encountered and there were more of Cain's oaths about the windups than the lamplight of the gospel. For what if people could manipulate events of the past? What harms could be done? What strange blessings contemplated? And with such an ability common among a people with all the contentions and foibles common to the Saints, what strange things might result? Many had obtained these entertainments, and the potential for confusion was profound if there were any truth to the matter. We stayed awake late into the night speaking of these uncanny events and renewed our commitment to visit the man that had inflicted such things upon the Saints.

27 June 1916
In the morning, I headed to up the Virgin River to where Mr. Bayes was known to camp. I suddenly wished that I had not been sent from Salt Lake to investigate this matter alone. Some help from other members of the Twelve with whom I might have consulted would have been beneficial at a time like this. I was terribly tired, for I had tossed and turned most of the night, troubled by the events of the previous day. I also wished I would have asked *all* the members not to use the machines until we could settle the matter of what they were or how Mr. Bayes was mesmerizing so many of the Saints.

The airship in which I rode was one of the newer models with a steam-driven propeller and helium in the bag chambers rather than the hydrogen that had proved so disastrous to the South during the Civil War.

Because the winds were contrary, I had some time before we reached our destination, so I pulled out the Doctrine and Covenants and read from Section 343. The verses therein had considerable value to me because the Prophet had read them to me on my last visit with him in the Emma Grand on North Temple. This would have been in 1890, right before his death. He was approaching eighty-five but his eyes were as clear as a much younger man's, and although his hand trembled just a bit as he took mine into his, his handshake was firm and hearty.

Brother Talmage, he said, smiling, *I've called you here because there is something I feel I must tell you, but my mind is slipping a bit and now, for the life of me, I cannot recall it.* His eyes drifted to the large oil painting above his head and I followed his gaze. It was painted by the German convert Udo Grimm depicting the Battle of Chickamauga in which Joseph Smith III had crushed the Confederate Army being led by General Braxton Bragg, changing the fortunes of the war. Of course, as is oft told, near the end of the battle a stray cannonball from his own regiment took Smith's life, one of the great tragedies of Church history because many believed that he would go on to lead the Church. Then he turned to me again and with tears in his eyes pulled the scriptures from his nightstand and read from the above-mentioned scripture, *"Wherefore, inasmuch as the Saints follow wisdom and seek to face the future with the faith and courage befitting the elect, no device formed against them shall prevail. Look forward. Fear not. The future is yours."* The Holy Prophet Joseph looked at me and said, *I have forgotten what I meant to tell you. I must rest. I'll call you again when I recall the matter.*

I assumed it had something to do with the newly founded Charles Darwin Academy where I was serving as president after earning my Ph.D. back East, but I never found out, for much to our sorrow he went downhill quickly, and by December had passed away, thus fulfilling the prophecy that he would not live past his eighty-fifth birthday.

I turned to the D&C and pondered the scripture that had been last read to me by the Prophet. It was about the future: the very thing at risk, was it not? Were these windups the devices to which the Lord referred?

It was nearly dark when I found Mr. Bayes's camp on the banks of the Virgin River. He was living in a small sheepherder's trailer equipped with large wagon wheels and a wood canopy painted white. A campfire was situated near the steps that led to the front door, and as I approached I was sure my eyes were playing tricks on me. The man I presumed to be Mr. Bayes was sitting on the steps that led to his trailer. He was a large man with massive hairy arms and a chest like a barrel. He had a flaming red beard that cascaded wildly to his breast and a mop of similarly colored hair, like the mane of a lion. But he made little impression on me because of the oddness of his companion standing near the fire, stirring a large pot. The man was diminutive. Smaller than a circus dwarf but proportioned more like a tiny full-grown man than a midget. He was as lithe as a willow but when stretched to full height stood only to just below my knee. His face was graceful and sharp; his eyes never seemed to cease darting around, settling nowhere, giving him an aspect of panicked and unblinking vigilance.

Mr. Bayes observed me for some time after my greeting him. Unlike his companion, his eyes weighed me with a steadiness and purpose that seemed to wrestle control of my will. I was forced to abandon my gaze upon him and turn my eyes firmly toward the ground before me.

You have come for a toy, he finally observed.

No, but I have come to inquire how they work, how they are made, and by what means you deceive people into believing their effects.

At my boldness, the little man stopped what he was doing and looked at me. Mr. Bayes roared with laughter. It was then that I observed a red ribbon running from Mr. Bayes to the small creature (I call him creature because the more I observed him, the less he appeared to be one of the sons of Adam). It bound their wrists together at a length of about thirty feet.

And who are you currently? he asked.

Despite the odd phrasing, I answered honestly. *I am Second Elder in the Church of the Firstborn of the Son, Keeper of the Elysian Mysteries, and Proconsul of New Ionian Sea City.*

Ah, he answered insolently. I regretted not having brought a shock of centurions with me to act as guard. In fact, it seemed especially odd that I had not. Normally, when I did the bidding of the governor I would have them with me.

Drink with me before you disappear in a poof of someone's wish and vanish into never having existed, the man commanded. His Latin seemed to be tinged with a lilt from the great Southern continent and I wondered if he was from the Sicilian continent below the narrow neck of land spoken of in the Book of Mormon. I had served a mission near the mouth of the Grand Po River and had travelled deep into the jungles that lined both banks of the mightiest river on the planet.

The man imbibed cup after cup of sour wine, the supply of which there seemed to be no end. I pretended to join him, but in reality I was tossing it into the sagebrush behind me. The little man observed my behavior several times but said nothing.

At last overcome by drink, Mr. Bayes began snoring heartily. I turned to the little man, who thus far had said nothing. He ignored me for a moment but gave several exploratory tugs on the ribbon that bound them, sighed, and then sat upon the ground.

Can you speak? I asked at last.

Of course, he said. *But it does me no good, so why bother? So what have you learned of the toys you're so curious about? Here, try one.* He reached into a large bag at the base of Mr. Bayes's wagon and handed me a small windup toy like those seen in ancient times. I watched him carefully as he handed it to me, looking for some clever prestidigitation, but I saw nothing out of the ordinary. The device depicted a hopping animal now long extinct after the nuclear war between the Norman and Roman Empires that had destroyed so much of the great island continent's fauna, including this hopparoo. I wound it up and it hopped around frantically. Almost as it finished, two Imperial jets screamed overhead, no doubt patrolling the air for Chinese incursions.

Have you a wish? I could not get over the strangeness of this fellow. His diminutive size. His strange dress, as if he had come from something out of an earlier era, maybe just after the first millennium of the Empire.

A wish? I have many. Right now I've been travelling for weeks on a monotonous exploration of this river system to find a suitable location for the new hydroelectric dam, I am fretting constantly over many beleaguered concerns, and I can think of nothing I wish more than to see my wife and children.

At that my wife turned to me and said, *Why in heaven's name would you wish that?*

I have to admit I was not sure why I had said it. My two children were poking sticks in the fire, pulling them out and waving the burning ends around following the glowing traces through the dark air. Sparks leapt from the flames and soared into the night sky.

I was a little embarrassed that I had said such a thing in front of my wife. The little man looked amused. He gave a couple of more tugs on the ribbon, but when the snoring Mr. Bayes popped his head up and mumbled something incoherent, he quickly let the line go slack.

I rewound the little toy and watched it once again dance about.

The little man took out a strange wooden stick and started speaking to it in a singsongy foreign language. It was strange and melodic.

How I wish I understood that beautiful language, I muttered, and he immediately switched to Latin.

Funny how these pockets of stability arise, he said. *With such drastic changes in the broader field you would expect that an individual would not survive, but the conditions of these are such that no one may end their own life, so to create the uniqueness of an existing life much temporal structure must be maintained or designed in such a way that survival is possible, like all the parents, and those communities that support the existence of that individual and all his predecessors. So despite radical large-scale changes, narrow lines remain consistent. Much like stirring a pot of noodles, as a mass they can be rearranged much, but the connection between two ends of a single noodle remain bound together no matter how tangled the mass becomes. We have given nearly two-dozen of the toys away in the small town, and yet much remains of these people's past, even though entire large-scale histories are in commotion. These stabilities intrigue me.*

It was apparent that I was in the presence of a demigod or daemon of some sort. Had not the Prophet warned us of such things?

I interrupted the creature's strange ramblings to find out more about its presence and intent. Clearly the windups were doing harm, but I had seen nothing that indicated harm other than the strangeness of a propensity or predilection to wish suddenly for what one already had.

How are you called? I asked.

He smiled and said nothing, so I tried another approach. *Why is there a ribbon between you and Mr. Bayes?*

He has learned my name and bound me. I am his servant. His slave.

Come now, man! The Empire banned slavery after the reforms of Caesar St. Stephen of Alemec at the Council of Alexandria in 984.

Of course, he said, *even so.*

You are not of this world. I said this with such certainty that I was surprised, for its realization came as the words were spoken.

It is worse than that, he laughed. I thought of the many science fictionals I had read as a young man. Tales of travel to another world. It was said that no one liked strange futuristic tales more than Joseph Smith as a boy. Indeed, the anti-Mormons are always trying to look for hints to the source of the Book of Mormon in Montaigne's *Star Dreamer* trilogy or in Sampson's *Ring of Bright Moon Rising,* two of Joseph's favorites. When his brother Alvin was killed in the Empire's space academy in a moon rocket accident, Joseph gave up the genre because it reminded him of his brother's death. But it is said he had read many as a lad.

I thought about the two desires I had expressed after each winding. I am not a slow man in general, but I had wished for the presence of my wife who had not left me and for understanding a language that is perfectly clear.

Do these play with time itself? I said, holding the toy for his inspection. He said nothing, but the knowing smirk that cut his narrow face was not hard to interpret.

It was dark. Cassiopeia was low in the northern sky. The snores of Mr. Bayes had reached a deep sonorous cadence and the stars were splashed across the sky in three dimensions. I thought of the inter-empire mission now hurdling its way through the sky toward Vega. Launched in 1906, it would reach there with its suspended crew in 1923. In the southern sky, the faint red glow from the eruption of 1892 that destroyed the town of Washington masked the stars of that region of the sky. My wife was sitting near the fire, joining the children in watching the blaze. She was reading to them from the Book of Mormon by the dim light of the fire, and they were staring at the coals frisking bright then dim in the errant breezes playing about the flames.

Those things that you have given away—People are wishing things right now, changing things as we speak. Am I right?

He shrugged again. *These are not my concerns. I care nothing for this place. Let someone wish that the Dark Ages never occurred, let someone's child wish to see a volcano, let someone in a fit of anger wish away their spouse. I don't care. Chaos is just around the corner.*

But we cannot cause our own death?

The daemon, for that is how I was beginning to think of him, look surprised and laughed. *So you understood me. How delightful.*

A panic was rising with his words. Wish my spouse away? How horrible, but could just an errant wish said in jest or consternation perhaps change everything? Change the fabric of time itself? Was it possible? Nothing seemed different from how I had always known things, yet a nagging and gnawing discomfort and fear seemed to be gathering around me, as if the world had an ersatz aspect. As if a second sense were steering me toward bleak conclusions, impossible yet gathering shape in the darkness of the night. The bound daemon and Bayes in his Etruscan skirt seemed to have about them a terror that was hard to describe or even see, like a bird discerned from the corner of one's eye as it darts from a bush: elusive, not completely entering one's gaze, yet real and hard to mistake.

I walked over to the fire and put my arm around my wife. I turned to the daemon and asked if my wife might not have one of the windups. From the bag he pulled a green tin frog, the key popping from its back like a tiny pair of fairy wings, and gave it to her.

She wound it up and placed it on the ground where it hopped frantically like a piece of dry ice on a griddle. She moved to say something but I placed my finger on her lips to suggest silence.

My dear, ask that these words I am writing be preserved.

Ask who? She looked at me and then at the sleeping man as if to ponder whether I had been drinking.

No one in particular. Just say it to the air.

She rolled her eyes. *Ok, let these writings be preserved, as is, forever and for all time. How was that?*

My son picked up the frog and, having wound it, watched as it jerked its legs about, hopping this way and that, until finally it bounded out of the light of the fire and into the darkness of the surrounding night. The moon was just setting over the rim of the canyon and the blackness was now held at bay only by the firelight. With the moon's departure the night had gotten quite dark. Even though it had been only at quarter stage, it had given a soft glow to the landscape.

It's too bad there are not two moons, my son said as he searched in the willowy area just out of reach of the fire light. *I would like that.*

Selene was just rising from the other rim and light returned to the valley. For some reason, Selene had always brought me more comfort than Luna, its irregularities and odd shape providing a better metaphor for humanity in all her weaknesses. The soft light of Selene was redolent of many a summer evening chasing fireflies as a child around the amphitheater at the Temple of Athena that Joseph the Prophet had built near Nephi's Landing.

But there was work to be done. If I understood things rightly, then my hopping toy had but one request left. A nonsensical request it would appear. But nonetheless.

Momentarily I will look over at the little man, the daemon, and say, *I wish that little monster had never been captured.*

President Smith, I found these notes on my person while at my desk this morning. Strangely, I also find I am wearing my traveling clothes and smell of campfire smoke. I will therefore be going home to change. I will be back this afternoon. Almost as if in a dream, I remember saying the very words that end this narrative, but cannot remember the context for having uttered them. I also have no memory of writing these notes, but as they are addressed to you I will forward them accordingly. President, I am quite shocked at their contents. I do not remember writing them, but it is in my pen. The narrative makes no sense and seems like something more akin to H. G. Wells than any report in which I have been asked to take part. I must say that the joke is on me; whomsoever is having this bit of fun at my expense has mastered my hand in almost every particular. So, in short, I am likely forwarding someone else's frivolity. I have not time to be part of whatever this is meant to be. I suspect it is B. H. Roberts and I will confront him at the first opportunity. But I send them to you, President Smith, to do with as you see fit.

Recreated in His Image

D R. MAMUND FLIPS THROUGH THE PATIENT'S CHART while taking a drag from his Jasmine Light.

"You know," he comments, exhaling the blue smoke into the surgery, "It's a pity to destroy art like this."

His nurse seems distracted, likely watching something subjectively in his visual field from the net.

"Nurse! Can you join me for a moment?"

The nurse snaps his attention back. "Sorry. Watching the match."

"And?"

"Cameroon is going down to Japan 2–3. What we got?"

"It's a damn shame, it's one of Asundra's sharks. Beautiful work. A natural-bred shark too. His Italian parents were both Asundra originals."

"She's the one who first engineered the exoskeleton crab claw onto a human arm, right? We studied her work in the gene art expression course when I was an undergraduate."

"Exactly. These sharks were earlier works, and for my money the best shark remap in the world. Her work will be mimicked for centuries. True genius is rare in this world. Ah well, we are all slaves to fashion, eh?" He shakes his head a little sadly, walks over to the happy-sunshine-surgeon, flips it on, and turning to the nurse says, "Send him in."

The nurse saunters toward the door, but turning her head calls back, "Japan scored."

The man she ushers in is a typical shark. Short, stocky, large barrel chest, two sets of fleshy caudal fins along his sides, and a small gorgeous dorsal fin protruding from his back. His face is classic Italian—dark complexion, with thick black hair. Only his incisors are shark-like, shining fiercely when he smiles. The man is a work of art. Dr. Mamund bites his lip. He is about to destroy it.

"Mr. Caetani, please sit down; we just need to go over some things to make sure you understand the procedure and see if you have any questions. All right?" The doctor puts his cigarette out and the air is automatically re-ionized and cleared.

The shark-man nods nervously.

"I understand you want to go back completely to an ancestral human look?"

"Yes. I want to honor what we came from. I'm a Mormon now and . . . well the old style body means something."

The doctor cannot help himself, it's not on his list of questions, but by damn he has some integrity left, and every once in a while he just has to say what is on his mind.

"Your parents were engineered by the gene artist Asundra, right? You were bred from their sperm and egg, right?"

The man shifts uncomfortably then says almost to himself, "Yes. My mother even carried me in her body until twenty weeks. She believed it helped her bond to me in ways that can't be had by an entirely in vitro pregnancy."

"And you are sure you want to take this away and . . ."

The man glares angrily, "Look. I've thought a lot about this. I've got a right to make a choice. Right? This is a matter of faith. I want to look like God. OK? Got it? I want to go old school humstyle."

The doctor shrugs. "Of course. Shall we continue? You've made arrangements to go online-virtual for the two weeks it will take, correct? You don't want to pop back into reality while this is going on.

It will be messy, painful, and affect every system in your body. You want to be somewhere else."

The man sighs, "Yes, my wife and I are taking our consciousness on an extended sci-fi mystery excursion slated to last the whole two weeks."

"You may want to go as an ancestral human in the Sim—to start adjusting to having that kind of body. It's very different."

The man looks away. "Yes, we thought of that too. Both my wife and I are going human form. My wife is thinking of making a change too, she's feline, and this will give her a chance to explore the decision. She's not a Mormon. Yet. But she's thinking about it."

"OK, then. Let me tell you what's going to happen. We are going to take off the fins mechanically; it makes the cellular rewrite easier. Then the nans are going to move into your cells and manipulate your DNA. We will snip out Asundra's work and replace it with straight-up, old-style human code. You've picked out the kind of genes you want, right? . . . yes, I see you have . . . good. Then the developmental code readers are going to take over and you are going to be remade—essentially a new skeletal and muscular structure and some minimal neurological rewiring. It's all automatic and rather boring mechanically. The risks are minimal, and you've been briefed and signed a release form I see . . . but you should be aware that some things might be surprising. Especially with artists like Asundra who were very nuanced and meticulous in their art."

"OK, yeah. I've been through all this with the counselor. I'm ready."

"Fine."

The doctor sighs. Defeated.

"OK, let's do it. If you will take off your robe and lie down on the operating table and go deep virtual we will get started."

The man climbs onto the operating table and lays down on his stomach, his large dorsal fin sticking into the air. As he relaxes visibly, the doctor reads the man's state: subjectively he has gone deep virtual.

The doctor walks over to the happy-sunshine-surgeon and taps a button on the screen. The machine goes to work immediately, dropping a shield over the prostrate man. The sound of saws cutting flesh follows within seconds, then the wet splashing of someone being lowered into an evo-rewrite chamber.

Dr. Mamund sits down in a recliner, lights a cigarette, and clicks the game into his visual field. Cameroon has scored again! This was anyone's game.

Runners

HE JUMPS INTO THE CAR. THE WHITE FROST COVER-
ing the windshield should hide him long enough to catch his breath. Thankfully, there is a key in the ignition. Rubbing his hands together, he blows on them, taking valuable time, but he can hardly make a fist, his fingers are so cold. The windows are frosted over inside as well as out, so he reaches past the steering wheel and rubs his bare palm hard against the glass to clear a small portal through the driver-side window. The ice is thinner in the arc the windshield traverses. An intact windshield, that's why he suspected it was a working car when he ran for it.

He hears a rustling and whips around, ready to dive from the vehicle and run. There is a young girl in the back seat, curled against the passenger side door. He stares for a second. She is alive. It's a complication, but one he can deal with.

He rolls down the window to get some grasp of the situation around him, then quickly rolls it back up. He is on the edge of town. Good. That will make it easier to get away.

The car is brittle cold and smells of onions and old motor oil and the locker room stink of people who have not bathed in a long time. He glances into the rearview mirror. The girl stares back briefly, then turns away; she's eight, maybe nine. She whimpers something he can't understand. He turns back to the problem at hand and twists the key hard. After some sluggish protest, the car groans to life. It's sputtering a bit, but it's good enough. It runs. He jams the car into drive and guns it out of the convenience store parking lot. As the car hits the gutter a large purse topples off the passenger seat into the assorted garbage that lies haphazardly on the floor—a scripture quad, old clothes, drink cups. He looks down; the handbag has disgorged a wallet slopping out several worthless credit cards. He catches a glimpse of a deer-eyed woman with long straight hair staring up from a driver's license. His eyes return to the road. There's not much time.

Somewhere beyond the darkening gray, the sun is setting.

He aims down the road, which is snowy but not icy, and roars onto the pavement, slipping between two cars. There had been enough traffic to wear a couple of black wet grooves. There are a few other cars. No one turns on their headlights. They are all going the same direction: away. Into the desert. He clicks the defrost on high, and slowly the little patch of transparency he opened on the windshield begins to grow. He settles down. The gas tank is nearly half full. That will help. He focuses on the late model yellow minivan in front of him. It's still light enough he can identify the "Families are Forever" bumper sticker. He knows he needs to see it without headlights when it gets dark. Concentrating on the car in front of him will make it easier to stay on the road as he tries to make it somewhere safe.

Somewhere safe. Funny.

He adjusts the mirror to consider the girl. She looks up and locks his eyes for just a second, but just as quickly looks away. She is curled against the door hugging her knees, shivering. There is thick dried blood around her nose. Her hair is matted on one side of her head; it looks like blood, but he knows it is not, just gunk. Maybe oil. Maybe mud. If it were a wound of that magnitude she would not be so alert. Anyway, how could she have gotten such a wound without being dead? Ergo she must not be wounded. Logic. He's got to hold on to that in the face of it all. She has no coat, but wears a horizontally striped shirt. Not torn or worn, just covered in dirt. She has deck shoes on her feet. No socks. She could not have been sitting here long. Not with the car parked, the heater off. She would have frozen to death. He looks at the large leather purse beside him, hoping to see a candy bar or some mints. He thinks about his food storage and a laugh bubbles up. Buckets of wheat. Useless. They hit the houses fast. There was not time for anything. Not even grabbing the seventy-two hour kits.

The car passes a billboard with a heroic father coming through the door with a pizza held aloft, his family cheering. He thinks about his son and daughter. His son, not much older than this girl in the back. His daughter, a toddler. He buries the thought before it goes too far. He can't think about some things right now. He looks back at the girl.

"Your mother is dead?"

It is barely a question. She doesn't answer. She doesn't need to.

He reaches into his large army coat and pulls out a .40 magnum S & W 4.5 inch. He hands it to the girl. "I need you to trust me."

She takes the gun, the first real sign that someone is home behind those hollow eyes.

"Do you know how to use it?"

She does not make eye contact and does not answer, but drops the clip out of the handle to check if it is loaded, then pushes it, hard, back into place. She knows how to use it. Of course she does. She places the gun on her lap and places her hands on top of it. Her eyes flick to his. She does not smile, but holds his gaze a little longer.

It is fully dark now. The stratus ceiling has a slight glow and he knows there must be a bright, nearly full moon somewhere in the sky. Out of habit, he turns on the radio and knobs through the stations. There is nothing, of course, but he goes through the motions.

As it darkens, he can just make out the minivan cruising in front of him. He can no longer read the bumper sticker and the vehicle's yellow color has turned to white in the natural light of the sky's glow. He keeps his distance in case they brake. No one is coming from the other way. Occasionally a car or a pickup roars around him and then vanishes into the shortened horizon of the night. Why hurry past this line of cars? Wastes gas. And besides, there may be as many dangers lying ahead as behind. He holds his speed.

The girl in the back is hard to make out now that the sun has set. He's certain she is not asleep, despite the heavy air of the now warm car.

"Do you have a name?"

No answer.

He tries another tack, "How many were there?"

She whimpers and speaks for the first time, "Six."

"They didn't see you." It was not a question.

Her voice is just a whisper as she answers it anyway. "No. They didn't see me."

A vision passes before his eyes. One constructed from elements of his own past, but recontextualized to be about the girl's mother. He sees a woman torn to pieces after drawing them away from the car that held her daughter. Sacrifice. We know what that means now, he thinks. He imagines the little girl sneaking a glimpse of her mother's death as she ducks below the seats. It is easy to picture in his mind. He's seen similar scenarios played out over and over.

"She wasn't my mother." The girl whispers this too.

Of course. They had been thrown together. How many strangers ago were her real parents killed? Is he the third? The ninth? The twentieth person she has travelled with?

"I'll take care of you now."

"I know . . . Okay."

That was the strange thing. Or at least it seemed strange because of the apocalyptic literature he'd read before this happened. People were supposed to be tearing each other apart. Hoarding food. Gunning down their neighbors to protect their limited supplies. But that's not the way it went down. Not this time. Life was too precious. Everyone took care of everyone. It had evolved like that almost instantly. Trusting people had been the only way to survive, but of course resources were not limited. Not with so many gone.

You could still find cans on store shelves. No one had been forced to dig into their wheat and beans.

It starts to snow but it is hard to tell without headlights. The road is completely visible now—a white path through the sagebrush landscape. The minivan, sloshing before him through the storm, seems a strange comfort. Perhaps it was just a screen, or hedge, of protection for what lay ahead, but he liked that it was there.

On they drive. He hears the girl's breathing steady and deepen. He smiles.

The car clock says it's about 3:00 AM when he sees a cascade of red lights blink on from the distance, disclosing cars breaking hundreds of yards ahead. He slams on his own brakes, sliding a little, but coming to a hurried stop. The girl bolts up, now wide-awake. She stares at him for direction. He does not hesitate but leaps from the car, whispering for the girl to follow.

"Hurry! Run."

She does. They plunge into the sagebrush to the left. He catches a glimpse of the people who had been driving in front of him also fleeing their car. The people he had been following now for hours are running into the desert parallel to him and the girl, along a line perpendicular to the road. They steer a course toward each other. They are a middle-aged couple carrying large packs in one hand and sleeping bags in the other. They come together running. An old Primary song bubbles up to the cadence of his flying feet. *Pioneer children screamed as they ran, and ran and ran and ran.*

He is amazed that the girl does not seem to tire, but runs with the three of them, holding onto the gun like a racing baton. After about twenty minutes they all stop to catch their breaths, everyone is keeping their eyes on the path they have just traversed, watching for motion. They see no others fleeing. A grave sign, but he dares hope they ran the other direction.

The older woman is staring blankly back at the road. Even from there they can hear the carnage. There are a few gunshots signaling suicides and death pacts. They maneuver quickly behind an out-cropping of rock and squat low. Out of sight.

The man with the pack stomps his feet and looks at the coatless girl. "We've got to get her in some warmer clothes."

The woman takes an emergency blanket out of her pack and spreads it on the ground; they all sit down on one end and wrap the other around their legs for warmth. The older man detaches a rolled-up wool army blanket cinched to the bottom of his pack and wraps it around the little girl's shoulders. They are silent. A car horn goes off, long and blaring, bellowing into the night. After about an hour, it dims and starts a long decline into silence.

The older man takes out a milk jug of water from his pack and offers them a drink. They each take a modest swallow, self-rationing, and pass it back to the man with the pack. He takes a small drink and then forces handfuls of powdery snow into the mouth of the bottle. He then puts the bottle under the blanket between his legs. The woman takes four candy bars out of a stash hidden in an inner pocket of her ski jacket and passes them around. The Snickers are soft and warm from her body and after eating them quickly, all four lick the paper wrapping vigorously to get every drop of chocolate. The jug is passed around again and they wash down their meal with another drink of the snow-cold water.

The clouds have broken up. Patches of stars appear now and then. The moon has set and the blackness of the sky highlights the cold, distant stars.

Just before dawn the girl falls asleep, the gun in her lap. Her travelling companion takes it and puts it in his pocket. He'll give it back to her if she wants it, but he doesn't think she will. She trusts him now. They've run together and that means something. Maybe everything.

The Captain Makes a Friend on the Day His Cravings and Listings Disappear

To AND FRO, FROM SIDE TO SIDE, THE PIRATE GHOST, Captain Long Shanks the Bloody (born 1707, Edinburgh Scotland; died 1761) swayed through the endowment room.

"Arg!" he said. And he meant it.

"Shush!" A respectable lady named Pricilla Buttercup (born 1847, Boston, Mass; died 1888) shushed at him. She also meant it.

The Captain's proxy baptism had gone well enough. Of course that had to do with water and anything that had to do with water smacked of the open sea and the feel of ocean spray on the face and feel of a soft rain in tropical latitudes. Ah, water he was fine with. But standing in the back with the other ghosts trying to pay attention to the words coming out of the loud speaker was like to kill him again.

"My dear man, will you hold still! I find your constant motion very distracting on this most important day of our eternal lives." This was said by Pricilla Buttercup with a frown making her otherwise pretty face look more like the carved wooden masks sold up and down the west coast of Africa.

"Arg, deepest 'pologies miss," he whispered, "but I gave up me ghost" (and here he chuckled at his joke) "during a squall off'n the coast of Barbados, an' aye, it t'were a storm t'be remembered! Brave

I was. Run'n as you see me now, sway'n back an' forth, shout'n orders to me crew as me lovely frigate rolled hard starboard and port and pitched for and aft like ter devil he's self was man'n ter winds. But seems ter state of me body t'were done imprinted these motions on me spirit, like me habit of rum an' tobacca that's been wi't me since I fell over the rail and t'were drown't in ter wat'ry grave."

"My good man! I must insist that you maintain the quiet that such occasion as this demands. I have waited a long time for me . . . oh dear . . . I mean *my* descendants to find and unlock the door to my eternal bliss. So please, I beg you, let me listen."

The pirate, still listing from one end of the endowment room to the other, took off his hat and bowed to the fine lady in acknowledgement of her request. An angel standing glorious and bright in the corner watching with a stern eye, glowed with sudden fierceness, then in a glowering voice like the thunder of breakers off the Spanish coast bellowed, "Get that cap back on your head!"

It then pointed a long finger which burned like a sun blazing hot on becalmed seas and added, "And not another word from you."

"Ahharrgg." The pirate grumbled under his breath (such as it was), "Back on me boat I'd have ye flogged an' . . ."

Both the comely Victorian woman and the magnificent angel turned to him with matching fingers across their lips, and in startling unison a gave an exasperated and vigorous, "Shush!!!"

With a sour look on his face, Captain Long Shanks the Bloody folded his arms and acquiesced to the demands of his unpleasant companions. He continued to tack across the holy space.

To take his mind off his contrary companions, he looked down at his descendant who was doing his work for him. What a disappointment. Where had the strength of his blood gone? Could that lily-livered, frail thing below him really be one of his own? He did not look manly enough to even climb into the rigging of a tall ship let alone wield a cutlass in a fair fight. He must of come out of that frail wench from Liverpool, either her or that pleasing thing in Los Sauces in the Canaries. But either way he was nothing that ought to have sprung from his loins. When in his long line of offspring had the vigor of his vital essence departed? He shook his head. He remembered that he was not supposed to judge things by the standards set during his lifetime. What was it that that missionary in the spirit prison had said, "Judge not, that ye be not judged." Wise words. Heaven knew he'd had enough repentance to do to bring him to this point. Look at that mousy man below. He floated nearby. The fellow was staring intently at the . . . what was it called . . . oh yes, "film." He felt a strange fondness for this weak specimen of manhood. Perhaps there were things about him that would redeem him? Had not he, one of the most fierce and monstrous men of the seven seas, been redeemed by the meekness of He who died on the rood?

The prissy lady who had been so quick to repeatedly shush him was floating nearby looking at him watch his descendent.

"You are quite fortunate, good sir, to have an actual blood relative doing this blessed work for you. The woman yonder carrying my name is of no relation and was given me by happenstance." She was smiling sadly, which gave her otherwise stern face a rather pleasant aspect.

"Aye. I ought t'count me blessings. Might be as much help fer this feller as is fer me soul? Shiver me timbers, I's start'n to like this landlubber."

The woman floated closer and looked closely at her rough fellow traveler. He squirmed under her gaze, but found it strangely pleasant.

"When this is over," she asked with surprising forwardness, "would you like to float around some of the paths in the Appalachian State Park? It's quite lovely in the fall and always rejuvenates."

He gave a sheepish smile, "They say that when this is over I won't be list'n from side to side nor crave'n ter rum. A goodly walk would be nice."

He almost removed his cap again, speaking to a proper lady and all, but a glance at the seraph reversed his hand.

Even so, why was the angel now smiling like a fool?

Forgotten Zero

Ancient Palestine

ELDER JOAO GONCALVES CAVALCANTI, WEARING period dress, approached the young man reverently. The man (if such he could be called), a Nazarene day-laborer working on the Roman construction of Sepphoris, sat facing a group that had gathered to hear him tell stories. He gestured to the blaze of red buttercups emerging after a rare couple of rainy days. Elder Cavalcanti could not understand Aramaic, but he could easily imagine what parable the teacher was imparting. The short man, deep desert brown, his clothes dirty and worn, his feet stained sorrel from the Levant clay, smiled at the Seventy who was now weeping. The young man walked over and squatted beside Elder Cavalcanti, opened a small pouch, and gave him some dark bread and a small piece of dried fish. Of course he would! Of course.

The older man gestured to the Jesuit monk beside him. "Ask him for me. Please."

Two Days Earlier; EJGC's Chronology

ELDER CAVALCANTI RUBS HIS HANDS THROUGH HIS white hair and tries to suggest through his scowl that he is not pleased with Brother Keebler's Graham Cracker®'s rationalization. But he can't put his finger on why it's wrong.

He gives the man a long, concerned look before starting. "Brother Cracker," he begins, but the brother interrupts him.

"I'm so sorry, Elder Cavalcanti, but you have to call me by my full name, 'Keebler's Graham Cracker.' When my parents got a sponsor for my name, the contract was very specific . . ."

"Yes, yes, I know. I'm just not used to . . . We don't do this in Brazil. Anyway, Brother Keebler's Graham Cracker, do you feel completely justified in your actions?"

"Well of course! I had a beer with the Prophet Joseph Smith! He asked me to have a beer with him. What was I supposed to do? Tell him I couldn't drink one because I was a member of his church?"

"First, this isn't *his* church. And second, what are you going to do when you're asked if you keep the Word of Wisdom in your next temple recommend interview?"

"I don't know! What would you have done?"

Elder Cavalcanti looks at the ground. He honestly doesn't know.

Things were getting more and more complicated. As the Seventy in charge of time-travel, he couldn't help but take this all very seriously. The Saints were getting into trouble more and more often as they entered situations that they just weren't ready for. He thought of poor Sister Eva Mailefihi, his neighbor in the Avenues. Was there ever a more pure and righteous soul? But she travels back to ancient Tonga to visit her ancestors and no one is wearing proper clothes, modesty has not been invented, and within just a few weeks she's gone completely *au naturel!* The stake Relief Society presidency of the Ensign Stake travelled back to talk her into coming back but their report was very discouraging. Very discouraging indeed.

Elder Cavalcanti didn't know what to do. He'd even talked to the venerable President Uchtdorf, but at age 187, despite being blessed with many transgenic refinements, his hale and hearty transmod frame was supporting a very wobbly mind. He had just patted Elder Cavalcanti on the head and said in German, "I'm sure you'll navigate this turbulence and keep us pointing at the proper runway for a safe landing."

Things were spinning out of control. Should he suggest they ban all time-travel? Designate certain destinations off limits? What should he do?

The Catholic Church had complete contractual control over visits to Palestine 45 BC–AD 100, won though some fierce bidding (including much against the LDS Church), and they demanded a contract be signed forbidding tourists from talking about what they saw and heard. If someone violated it, the penalties were swift, expensive, and ruinous, and the Vatican was vigilant in prosecuting those foolish enough to test them.

As Elder Cavalcanti signed the contract, he readied himself to ask the only person he knew might be able to help him. His mother had taught him that the Savior had spent years being taught by angels about everything there was to know.

"Everything," he had asked, "even quantum mechanics?"

"Everything!" she had snapped. He was about to put it to the test.

Ancient Palestine

THE JESUIT ASKED THE GALILEAN CAVALCANTI'S QUEStion. There were, of course, no words or even concepts for time-travel in Aramaic, so they had agreed on several culturally appropriate words, like, if those of the Kingdom of God ever gained control over the order of events, should they rearrange them before they happened?

The Exemplar asked several no doubt clarifying questions, then answered the monk at length, all the while looking at Elder Cavalcanti as if he understood that it was *his* question. The Master then helped the Seventy to his trembling feet, grasped him by his upper arm, kissed him, and then began walking with his followers down the dusty road.

The monk looked at his charge and said, "He said you are crazy and have a demon. You should go to Jerusalem where there are many healers."

"But . . ." Elder Cavalcanti stammered.

As they walked back to the time-transfer point, the poor Seventy's mind was numb. What had happened? Obviously his mother was not correct about Christ and quantum mechanics, but he felt strangely sad and disappointed.

Suddenly, a woman that Elder Cavalcanti recognized as the pilot of their time machine came running up shouting and waving, "I'm so sorry. I've made a terrible error. This is A D 3, not A D 30! I'll get you a full refund."

"Who was that we spoke to?" the seventy asked the monk, feeling silly.

"A day-laborer, I suppose. Didn't know much about your problem, did he?" the friar said, not unkindly.

"No," Elder Cavalcanti said thoughtfully, "but he's helped me realize something nonetheless."

Time-travel has its perils.

Question Four

QUESTION FOUR IS COMPLEX.
It was the escape of the dog-faced baboon that first launched me into the more peaceful enterprise of capital 'S' Science.

Oddly enough, even now I find myself longing for the silent thrill of sneaking into the beast's cage, the smell of rank musk reminding me that mortality's end (or eternity's beginning) sat sleeping only one too-loud-a-footstep away. In those days I was a short sentence man, writing with curt, sudden jabs that poked through the ambivalent second-guessing that surrounds, or rather defines, our postmodern confusion and timid uncertainty. The baboon knew something remarkable, of that I was sure (see, even today short sentences sneak through like a husband returning to a theater line where he left his wife standing as he drove through blocks of crowded streets looking for a place to park but—not finding one—parks far away in a dangerous area, inviting unlooked-for worries as he runs through dark streets hoping that the line has not started moving). The truth is this: during the day, the beast would stare contemplatively (confidently wise (its eyes searching my face, penetrating my soul (or at least some biological subset thereof))) and then, slowly, with deliberate aloofness, nod knowingly, its slowly closing eyes bringing to mind a Buddhist monk bringing the day's teaching to a close. In the ape povillion, I tried to talk with it, like I did as a missionary, but like so many of those upon whose door

I knocked, it would feign indifference and disdainfully move on all fours to the furthest corner of its enclosure where it would nonchalantly gnaw a stick of sugarcane, leaving me alone to ponder the growing certainty that this simian was waiting to tell me something magnificent—an idea perhaps bigger than the solar system, maybe even bigger than the galaxy (I dared not extrapolate the idea further (such mistakes are often fatal (or, as all things are temporary (except perhaps the generations of Antarctic flies that have bred there secretly since the breakup of Gondwanaland) I mean immediately deadly) to the sane (did I mention I am sane? (Quite))) and would go no further even if my mind had allowed it). I knew that I had to find out what was locked away in those silent eyes, so beguiling and so unfathomable and so full of the power and spirit of the holy. My first attempt was on a night when the moon was as full as a plate of Antonio's steaming spaghetti, with garlic sauce (not too heavy on the cheese), because it's then that the guards are most easily avoided. Convinced that they can discern any ill, they stand in little groups, talking, glancing around occasionally while finding comfort in one another's boredom. Why do they need comfort? Because at night, the zoo comes alive with unearthly calls, moans, grunts, hacks, snorts, cackles, hoots, barks, cries, clicks, roars, peeps, slurps, yells, and a hundred other voices that do not belong in the city—voices that condemn it with their unrepentant music. With the silence of a lizard stalking a tenebrionid beetle in the lonely desert of the Southwest (a living-room motif I despise), I crept over a wall, through an enclosure holding timid and frightened flamingos, and then onto the roof of the ape pavilion where a bold rappel brought me into the beast's cage. But the untroubled creature slept through it all. And I, too awed to rouse it from its dreams of freedom, left (again annoying the flamingos, forcing them to grudgingly stand on two legs as their heads rose derisively from under their wings). Later, during my second attempt, the story was no different, except the moon was blocked by thick clouds from a summer thunder shower which had forced the guards to be more alert while the flamingos took less notice. And the baboon? It was sleeping badly—the thunder reminding it of carefree days spent playing in the savannah of Tanzania, capering near its caring mother's vocalizations. I remember nothing of the moon on the third try, nor of the upside-down smile of the flamingoes, nor even of the bored and sleepy guards, marching methodically down deserted trails, which glowed like miniature runways in the light of miniature electric lanterns in this miniature habitat. I only remember standing in the cage staring at the cool black eyes of the wakeful animal, finally aware of my benign intrusion. It moved to the corner opposite mine and stared at me like a beagle watching her master open a can of meaty dog food. I was tempted to think that it would finally share the secret that had brought me again and again and again and again to the window of its incarceration. I squatted down and, like a humble inductee of a pagan temple, begged to begin training, and with deep sincerity asked to be allowed to take him as my master and teacher. Suddenly, he began speaking in long, intelligible sentences (the kind I am trying to imitate here), and after emphasizing each point by slapping the floor with his open hands, he began a series of low grunts and menacing howls, the message of which my uncomprehending ears could not grasp—so unfathomable and poignant their meaning. In anger at my stupidity, he rushed at me as I tried to flee up the rope, but he took the end and shook it with such violence that I was forced to jump to the floor of his straw-filled enclosure. (And can I say here that I returned to prayer and to the view of a God who finds lost keys and cares if I pass my driver's test or whether I have Lucky Charms or Wheaties for breakfast—which place I had not been for too, too long?). He never looked at me again, but in a moment he was gone, taking my rope with him and disappearing so completely that neither the police, nor the sheriff's office, nor the division of animal control, nor Dr. Tillman of the University Center for Primate Studies, nor the zoo, nor Madame Bornatelli from the psychic hotline, nor Chett the purebred bloodhound from the State Prison System, nor neighborhood kids in five cities, nor the Channel 5

News helicopter, nor Mike Singing Eagle the tracker, nor twelve sets of Mormon missionaries called to help through my connections with the mission president, ever found him. People all over the state claim to have seen him stealing dog food or traveling in a Winnebago (sometimes with one of the Beach Boys) or have caught a fleeting glimpse of him crossing a lonely stretch of road on starry nights just as a fading radio station is being lost to increasing interference and the search for a new channel has begun; or have heard his cry as they sit near a dying campfire, in which the coals have burned low and a chill sneaks in, inviting thoughts of a warm sleeping bag; or have cited him as an explanation of a downed clothes line or overturned garbage can. All I know is that I was left alone to ponder my inept unworthiness at ever grasping the great secrets that he might have imparted had I been a more fit candidate or more prepared supplicant. As I sat bathed in regret, I saw the roaches, sitting thoughtfully just out of reach on the rough surface of the cinder blocks that fashioned my newfound prison. Their dark eyes were alight with the glow of the street lamps that patterned the walls like the straight lines of a cubist painting, perhaps a Gris or a Braque (you can choose) and cast deep shadows that seemed to enlarge the silent insects, giving them a presence far beyond the simple contours defined by their chitin bodies. Their noble antennae moved like the baton of a conductor playing freely with an orchestra (constrained neither by score nor budget), which gave them an air of courage and freedom that not even this frightful gulag could contain. It came to me like a comet from the heavens, like a first vision, like a motorcycle policeman from behind a billboard or perhaps a salesman at an electronics store, that the baboon had been nothing more than a vehicle for a greater wisdom. It was only a vessel filled from a fountain of greater purity, a springboard to an even higher consciousness of which the beast had been but a pupil, a novice, a beginner (it was in these great winged insects that the greater secrets were hidden, where the knowledge of the universe began)! I clapped my hands in delight, all the while recognizing that I was setting out on a more difficult sojourn than communicating with the baboon had ever been. I sat in thought until morning when I was found, arrested, and released. But as I carried my shoe hiding the timid blattids (which no one moved to take from me (neither did anyone seem to care that I preferred to walk with only one shoe)), I felt the birth of a new and higher quest.

This clearly answers Question Four: "Why do you want to pursue graduate study in entomology?" Question five: "What made you choose our academic program?" is complex and has less to do with the dog-faced baboon than with my dreams of smelting precious metals and your school's name spelled backwards using the Cyrillic alphabet and held to a mirror.

Part II

This World

Exactness

STAKE PRESIDENT NICHOLAS LINVILLE SAT STERN and still, weighing the bishop by the full measure of his authority—not masking disappointment, mind you, but still letting the edges of his compassion leak through his uncompromising standards of righteousness. The bishop had disappointed, true, but a bit of reproving with sharpness was probably enough to do the trick.

Bishop Timmons had proven himself a capable and compassionate leader. President Nicholas had few complaints about his service. Even so, the bishop was not a strong leader. He had a tendency to let the rules slip into insidious grays—no, not gray: there was no such color where the gospel was concerned. If the rules were not laid down in some detail, Bishop Timmons would choose a course of action that leaned away from the clear and unambiguous light toward the shadier side of whatever question lay before him. Such was this case.

President Nicholas eyed the bishop a little more closely. It was time to ask the penetrating question that would expose the bishop's error in all its insidious hues, exposing his crimes to the light.

"So let me get this straight. You did not see the massive case sitting by the piano?"

"No. My wife knows I'm just not that observant. It's a fault and a weakness I can't seem to correct."

"And why does the Lord give us weaknesses?"

"To turn them into strengths."

"Exactly. Here is the greater concern. When the girls pulled the instrument from its case you did nothing to stop it? You, who were presiding at the meeting, let them pull a *banjo* from the case and then sing a song . . . in *sacrament* meeting . . . that was *not* in the hymnbook? Please explain what was going through your head. Why was the appropriate action not taken?"

The stake president smiled inwardly. He listened to the excuses—how the Laurels had worked so hard to prepare, how they were all good girls, how he didn't want to disrupt the meeting, how it would have hurt the girls' feelings—especially the one who was less active, who was just coming back to church, how he thought he could correct them privately so it would not happen again, how the song—something about the master's hands—had actually moved people. On and on. Excuses. What excuses will he offer when he stands before the bar of the Holy One of Israel at the Great Judgment Seat? President Linville took a breath and began the reproving. It felt good to pull a brother back onto the straight and narrow.

It was a sad occasion. Funerals were always sorrowful meetings, but it was especially unfortunate when the die-ee had not quite been rigorous in keeping his testimony bright. President Linville looked down from his seat on the stand at the now widowed Sister Bain and shook his head. Brother Bain had been a hard man to figure out. He served as the elder's quorum instructor well enough and many had thought that he ought to have been moved into the high priests when he turned sixty-five. President Linville knew, however, that advancement in the priesthood was not conditioned on age. Brother Bain believed in evolution, despite his being given a copy of President Joseph Fielding Smith's *Man: His Origin and Destiny*. If a man will not see reason, there is no hope he can be pulled from the devil's grasp.

Bishop Timmons was conducting and had just arisen to introduce the next part of the funeral.

"Thank you, Sister Fuentes. That was a beautiful remembrance of your brother. Now the family has prepared a special musical number from one of Brother Bain's favorite songs."

Songs? President Linville looked quickly around to ensure (given the bishop's history on the matter) that there were no banjos hidden somewhere. Thankfully, he saw none.

A middle-aged sister came forward and stood at the microphone. She nodded to a man at the piano, who started to play. She began to sing Carole King's song, *"My life has been a tapestry . . ."*

The stake president gasped. This was a hippy song his kids had played over and over when they were growing up! He knew it well and even kind of liked it, but the chapel was no place . . . It got worse! From out of the foyer came a procession, with violins (that's fine) but the third person had a tambourine! Percussion! No. No. No. The song was continuing and people were standing in the audience joining in singing different parts . . . like a . . . like a . . . what was the word . . . "Flash Mob!" A flash mob in the chapel?

The song continued. King's lyrics brought such pathos and beauty. Yet it was completely inappropriate! President Linville looked at the bishop. Was he not going to stop this?

Then it happened. It took a few seconds to find where the noise was coming from: a young man standing somewhat hidden in front of the sacrament table playing an electric guitar. A guitar solo. A beautiful, haunting solo. Filled with all the depth and pathos that death could muster. It was beautiful. But . . . It couldn't . . . but . . .

He rose and walked to the sister at the mic. He had to stop this. Instead, with tears running down his face, and completely to his surprise and horror, he found himself singing with her, his hand thumping at his side in rhythm to the tambourine. And rather than censure, his big bass filled the chapel with one of the greatest songs ever written.

When the Bishop Started Killing Dogs

I T'S FUNNY WHAT MAKES A MAN GO CRAZY, BUT ONE thing is sure, no one expects it to be the ward bishop. It was Sunday morning and I noticed the police cars down the street at the Mullers'. Liz and I ran over to see what was going on. In our town when you see a police car at a neighbor's yard you zip over because you know who it is that lives there. Plus we are all in the same ward. When we got there it was plain to see what had happened. On their front lawn was their dog dead and with an arrow stuck in its chest. The officer was pulling it out and we could all see that it had a target tip and not a hunting tip and I think we were all a little surprised. It popped into our heads that this must have been teenagers because who else would have used a target tip when you want to take something down? The Muller kids were all crying and Sister Muller was crying too but she was evil faced and angry and was yelling Who would have done this?

Well, if truth be told, any of us could of done it because that dog barked all night every night. It was the bishop that actually done it. But we didn't know that and up he walked. Sorrowful and full of concern. He put his arm around Sister Muller and then squatted down on his haunches and talked to the kids. The police were asking if anyone had heard anything like squealing tires or seen kids out and about late but no one heard or saw nothing. Then Sister Keeling came over and said it's about time someone silenced that damn dog. The officer looked at her lowly with narrow eyes but then realized if she was the one that done it she wouldn't be so vocal and that it was just old lady talk. He just steered her back to the sidewalk because she was upsetting those that just lost the dog.

Animal control came. The same ones that scoop up the raccoons and deer that meet up with traffic. They picked up the dog and placed it tenderly in the back of their covered 4x4. I don't think they really cared but they made a good show of it for the kids and said they would make sure it got a proper burial but we all knew it was heading for the dump.

We shook our heads and chatted and wondered who would have done such a thing. The officer asked who had bows but of course we all had bows or at least a good number of us had one for the kids to shoot birds and squirrels with. And he acknowledged that an animal death would not be the kind of situation that would allow much manpower put to it. The bishop came up to Liz who was the Relief Society president and asked that she see that someone brought them some meals for the next couple of days. It was an upsetting thing for someone to murder your dog and a hot meal might be mighty appreciated at such a time.

What happened was this. The bishop who had been up for several nights cause of the barking dog and the worries on his mind for the ward's troubles couldn't stand it no more. He lives just two houses down and what with all the people's sins he carried in his heart with no way to let them out and that dog barking barking barking set his mind on fire. He could not tolerate it anymore and got up grabbed his grown up kid's old bow and snuck out in his PJs and pegged the dog from up close.

Of course it wasn't but two days later that the Mullers got themselves a beagle puppy. And damn it wouldn't you know but they set that thing outside and it whined and cried all night. It's like the Mullers are stone deaf. But the bishop having done it once did it again. On the third night they awoke to find dog number two shot through the eye with another target arrow.

Now the neighborhood was in an uproar. It was one thing for a bunch of wild teenagers to do something unbecoming one time random like but now people were kind of scared. Terrible rumors were arising about the last days.

The Mullers got themselves another puppy but this time they got a little terrier and kept it indoors. If you got close you could hear it whining inside the house but you had to get close so the bishop didn't kill this one. Without the Muller's dog barking it was downright peaceful.

Except for Brother Wain's old German shepherd lab mix. Now it was a little more sensible dog and didn't really bark except when it suspected there was mischief about. Still it seemed like there was mischief about often enough. Especially on fall nights when the wind blows out of the southwest. The skies are clear and it seems a little warmer than is proper for autumn. Something about all the trees knocking together and loose things people kept about their porches clanking and clicking would set that good dog to warning folks of the dangers it sensed riding in on the weather. We had quite a spell of this sort of thing and it seemed like that dog was sounding off four maybe five times a night for nearly a week. And the bishop having given into temptation before succumbed again. But this time he didn't use a bow.

Brother Wain told me he woke up to find his dog hardly able to catch its breath and dry heaving and choking. He tried to give it some water but then thinking something was really wrong drove it to the vet. It only survived about two hours. Brother Wain said the dog vet wasn't there being on vacation and the cow vet didn't really know what to do. He tried some things but they didn't work and the dog died. When the cow vet opened the poor thing's stomach he told Brother Wain that it was clear as water what happened. There was a chuck of hamburger and bacon all balled up around a center of D-Con rat poison.

Now three dead dogs was too many and folks got serious. I myself would get up three or four times a night and peer out the windows to see what was afoot. I never saw anything. We took to letting our dog sleep in the utility-room .

On Sunday the bishop stood up and with a smile welcomed us all. You would never guess what he was about at night. He told us that these were troubled times. He told us that the last days were here and that we should expect trouble. He told us also that he had a feeling though from the Lord that things were settling down and that we ought not to worry. The Lord would protect us and our animals. This I must say brought a measure of peace to the whole ward. I quit getting up at night and for all winter and most of the summer there was no trouble but of the usual kind.

By then the Mullers had kicked their terrier outside and them people who don't hear their own dog barking did not notice their dog was again keeping people up all night. Then one night we heard a ruckus. A bad wounded dog is a frightful thing to hear and even a little terrier can make a hellacious noise such as to make your teeth bleed in sympathy. All the kids were out of bed crying and I looked out the window and every house in the neighborhood was lighting up. It was 4:34 AM. I remember cause I looked at the clock. Then I seen him. Running low down. Bow in hand. White as a ghost. The bishop stealing from bush to bush, his big pot-belly and his bow legs making him easy to recognize. I threw on my pants and ran down stairs and made myself to the Mullers where a group of neighbors was gathered. I wasn't alone in seeing the bishop. Brother Hassenbach saw him too.

The terrier had been gut shot. This time with a four-sided hunting arrow which the bishop had picked up special showing how premeditated this round of death dealing was. The arrow had not hit the heart or vitals and had just spilled the poor dog's guts on the ground leaving his lungs free to mount the agony we had all heard. Brother Fisk put it out of its misery with a shot from his .357 Ruger Blackhawk.

Well the police came. Me and Brother Hassenbach told what we saw and they arrested the bishop. He confessed to the whole thing and was charged with misdemeanor animal cruelty him being friends with the judge and the prosecutor on account of his paint business. But the stake released him from being bishop even though besides killing the dogs he had been mostly a fine bishop.

I'm the bishop now. I've got troubles keeping me up at night and the new mutt the Mullers have brought home is barking up a storm. I'm thinking about it.

I'm thinking about it.

The Problem

THE BISHOP'S TONGUE IS THICK AND DRY FROM THE fast. His voice comes attended with a soft, sticky click as he sets the sister apart. Her hair is soft and slightly damp, not long from the shower. It smells like strawberries—not real ones. He attends to her small head cupped tenderly in his hands, the tip of his pinky resting on her ear, another contacting her temple. He can hear, or perhaps just sense, her breathing. Slowly. In and out. She is relaxed, soft. He can perceive easily her expectation and anticipation. As he blesses her that she will find joy in the service of her new calling, he can feel her neck stiffen as it tries to find an equilibrium in order to balance the heavy hands that weigh down her graciously bowed head.

The scent of strawberries returns. He beats down the fragrance. He becomes aware that he can feel certain aspects of her scalp— the coolness of her thin, blond hair; the firmness of her cranium; a slight indentation on the crown. He should not be so aware of her! Trying to relocate his attention, he continues after a pause. In and out. She breathes too deeply. He can hear her exhalations. He pauses again. Reorienting. He continues, saying that her husband, whose hands rest atop his, and that their children, all sitting reverently in four chairs lining the front of the office, will be cared for and blessed by her service. He feels stronger. More oriented. He focuses on her husband's large hands atop his. He admonishes her to seek the spirit in all things and he notices a sob, then a shudder under his hands, forcing a cascade of adjustment among the many hands as they renegotiate their strategic placement on her feminine crown. Her head becomes present to him again. He is made aware, once again, of the warmth and coolness of her gentle head. He feels drawn to her. Drawn to the sensation of strawberries.

"Thank you," she sobs.

Her husband holds out his hand and shakes Bishop Klaus's firmly. Nodding once with shining, watery eyes, "It was a fine blessing," he says, blinking.

They file out of his office, wife and husband, each with a young child on an arm and one in tow behind.

His clerk, Brother Thane, pops his head in saying he is going to run home and pick up his family. The bishop nods and returns to the leather chair behind his desk as the door softly clicks closed. He has fifteen minutes before sacrament meeting starts.

Dear Heavenly Father, please help me.

He had been a bishop for three years now and it had never been like this. Sure the occasional sister had caught his eye. But he had always been able to shift focus. *If you don't look once, you're not a man . . .* and all that. But now? What was happening?

To have these kinds of feelings during a blessing? What could be worse? It was getting bad.

These crimes were adding up. In PEC today, he had not been able to take his eyes off of Sister McInnis. She laughed so delightfully! She seemed to fill the air with pleasantness and light. Expressing concern over the Haungs so earnestly. Her every move seemed bathed in radiance. The curve of her neck was accentuated with off-white pearls; the soft hairs on her nape were playfully disordered, twisting loosely up to where her creamy skin was exposed, white, between her delicate ears and the end of her collar-bone, naked and pale in the office light—all of these distracted and damned him. Then, to get away from this fascination, he looked down, and to his consternation, his gaze fell on her ankle. It was wrapped in the straps of her white sandals that exposed her toenails and taunted his efforts to escape her neck. Oh no.

Stop! he called, almost aloud, pulling his eyes to just above her head, pinning them to the blackboard framed above her, where the names and pictures of the twenty-four primary children he was trying to memorize were pasted. He tried to listen as Brother Hack, the ward mission leader, was rambling on about the Giffords, a part-member family he was working with. But Sister McInnis's neck would not leave him alone. It was so . . . so present!

And it wasn't just Sister McInnis. The other night, it was Sister Wray, the Young Women's leader. She had caught him in the hall just outside the auditorium on activity night last week.

"Bishop Klaus!"

She was dressed for yoga. The Young Women were having a demonstration from a neighbor of Sister Tanner from the Franklin Ward. The Young Women leader's hair was tied in a ponytail, and she was dressed in loose T-shirt and grey sweatpants tied in the front. He stared at her in horror. She looked so cuddly. So soft and curvy.

"Bishop Klaus?"

"Sister Wray! What can I do for you?" His eyes locked on hers. He would not look down.

"I need to talk to you."

She stepped closer. She smelled like baby powder. She said softly, almost whispering, "It's about Melissa. I think she is in more trouble than we thought. Can I talk to you after Young Women's? She's missed the last four activities."

The bishop allowed concern to bubble into his face. "Yes, of course. Come by after your meeting."

When she came into his office, she was red-faced and slightly sweaty from her workout.

"I'm sorry to look like this."

He noticed she said "sorry" in the Canadian way.

"Please, don't give it a thought. How are you holding up?" She seemed grateful for the question.

"Derrik's new job is keeping him busy, and the boys never let up, but I'm doing OK. I guess."

"You are doing a terrific job. My daughter loves your classes and raves about the activities. You are very deeply appreciated."

She smiled, humbly. "Thank you, Bishop. Your daughter is such a sweetheart. I wish Melissa were as active. I'm not sure what's wrong. She used to come every week, but . . . well, she's got a new boyfriend and she hasn't been here for a while, and with her mother having taken her name off the rolls . . . I'm just worried."

Bishop Klaus had not heard a word. Sweat had soaked the collar of Sister Wray's T-shirt and the ring of moisture had pulled him completely out of the conversation. It took him a moment, but he reconstructed the gist of her words.

He smiled, but it felt creepy and uncomfortable, as if he had just been caught doing something unsavory. He worried he was leering.

"I'll talk to Melissa. Her mother, I'm sure, deep down knows the truth and is being blinded by the sophistries of men. I'm convinced she'll come back. But I'll talk to Melissa. Her dad is one of the good guys and I'm sure he's doing all he can to hold his family together. For some reason Satan wants that family bad, but we aren't going to let him have them."

Sister Wray tightened her lips and nodded with determination. "My goodness," she said, "look at me, I'm sweating like a wildebeest! I'll let you go. I know how busy you are."

He rose and shook her hand. "I *will* look into it." She had hesitated to take his hand, just for an instant, and although he was sure it was because she was damp and overheated, he couldn't help but wonder if she had caught something inappropriate in his gaze.

Sacrament had gone OK, but not great. He had wisely chosen to put the podium between himself and Sister Galliano who always had a neckline that was too low, exposing dark, tan cleavage, the freckles of which seemed to pull his eyes down almost of their own accord. He had to get her to the temple soon, even if her husband had not quite given up coffee yet. But he had not counted on Widow Gorse's daughter-in-law in the front row. A non-member, her skirt was showing way too much thigh and he had had to spend much of the meeting reading the text of hymns.

Bishop Klaus was in agony by the time the day was done. He told the clerk that he would lock up himself. He made his rounds, making sure the building was empty and that he was alone. Then he retreated to the chapel. It was dark and a little strange. It felt too empty, how busy it was during meetings. He made his way past the rows of benches and stood before the white tablecloth of the sacrament table—which the teachers had neglected to fold and put away. He got on his knees in front of that sacred board. He wanted to pray, but he felt dirty. Tainted. That's why he had chosen this place in the chapel. This is where the deacon's feet would stand to take the trays. He wanted to acknowledge his depravity. His humility. His need for help. He started his prayer, "Our Heavenly Father," but his mind wandered. Why was this happening? He loved his wife. She was everything he could ask for. They had a fine sex life, especially in light of some of the stories he was hearing among some ward members he was counseling. So why was every woman he met suddenly so attractive?

He continued his prayer, getting the thank-yous out of the way so that he could pour his heart out. But the words wouldn't come. He cried for help, but the heavens were brass, as they say. Nothing was getting through. His words sounded hollow and empty. These were the Last Days. Was that it? Did the daughters of Zion dress too provocatively? Was he being drawn away by the very things that Isaiah had warned about? The prancing? The mincing? He tried to shift the blame to the women, but even as he made the move, he recognized that, no, it wasn't them. It was him. They had always dressed this way. It was he who had changed. He struggled to find purchase on a place from where he could plead for help. But there was nothing. He sighed and struggled to his feet.

Then, clearly, suddenly, to his mind the words "YOU, TOO, SHALL FALL" were presented with such force that he looked up expecting to see Heavenly Father staring at him, fierce and angry. But it was dark. And silent. The headlights of a passing car bled through the curtains, momentarily causing the sacrament table to glow, creating a fleet of shadows that moved quickly across the chapel. Then it was dark again. He felt sick.

He would not fall! He marched resolutely towards the exit. "I will not fall," he repeated aloud. He left the building and walked the mile and a half home. He would not fall. He would not fall!

That week after PEC, however, he was vaulted back into despair. Sister McInnis had looked stunning. She had cut her hair, lifting it off her neck a little more. She was wearing black beads and long diamond earrings that dangled half way down her neck. He had been determined not to look at her. And he had done so well—until the elders quorum president started droning on about the lack of enthusiasm the elders were showing for cleaning the building on Saturday nights. The bishop's mind had started wandering and before he even realized it, he was staring at her again! But what was worse, when he looked up, Brother Martin the high priest group leader was glaring at him. From then on, he only looked at her when she was talking and then only into her eyes. Oh, my. Her eyes. Her long lashes . . .

No! He shook himself. He was angry. Angry at her. Angry at the high priests group leader. Angry at the elders quorum president. Angry at everyone. This was getting out of control. It had to stop. He could feel a fury taking over.

His clerk popped his head in.

"Brother Connors is here."

Brother Connors was always here. Every third week Brother Connors was here. His pattern was as predictable as car commercials during the nightly news. Pornography. One week he would come in despairing, crying to the bishop about falling off the wagon again. Then the bishop would counsel him, encourage him, lift him. They would pray together, read some scriptures together, pray again asking Heavenly Father to bless the man with strength. Then he would leave. He would make it a week, reading his scriptures as the bishop had advised when he felt tempted. But then, after a week, maybe two, he would get on the computer late at night, and then back into the bishop's office. Over and over, the same thing.

"Show him in," he sighed. His teeth were clenched, his knee bouncing in agitation.

Brother Connors came in shamefaced. He sat on the chair across his desk looking at the floor.

"What happened, Bill?" The bishop tried to keep his voice even."

Brother Connors began to relate his story. The bishop could not focus. His mind wandered. The story involved driving past a strip club and deciding to take a peek. Suddenly Bishop Klaus began to imagine Sister McInnis in a strip club. Dancing on a pole like he'd seen on a TV show that had gone places a family show should not have gone.

"NO!" Why was this playing through his mind? Why did he have to listen to this? Brother Connors was not going to change. He was nothing but a weak man. He was going to fall away again and again. There was no end to this. YOU TOO SHALL FALL.

"NO!" He didn't mean to say it out loud. He didn't mean to shout it so loudly. But once it was out. He couldn't stop himself. And he just unloaded. It all spilled out of him with vehemence. He couldn't seem to control it. He was surprised to find he was shouting, but it kept coming. He kept shouting. It was almost like he was watching a movie of himself over which he had no control.

"You weak little man! You coward! Why do you keep returning like a dog to its vomit? Every damn week it seems like you're here, telling me how you could not live up to your covenants, how the 'temptations' 'overwhelm' you and you just can't seem to control it!

Do you think this doesn't affect your relationship with your wife! Do you think you can just keep repenting and then coming in here and wasting my time with what you clearly have no interest in changing? You can't resist? You can't control it? You can't get a handle on it? You don't even *try!* It's only been three weeks! Three weeks! And you can't even control it that long before you are in here again shamefaced begging the Lord's and my forgiveness? We can all control our minds! We have that power! We don't have to fall into this. We don't have to fall! Do you understand me? We don't have to fall! You can't just stare at women as if they are objects for our lust! Do you understand me? It takes the Spirit away! It spoils everything. You think you can just sit there and stare at their neck and ears without drawing down the ire of heaven? What if that woman sitting there were Heavenly Mother? Would you lust then? We can't just keep letting these uncontrollable urges take us away from the spiritual responsibilities we have been given! Do you understand me! DO YOU! You can't go on like this. You are not going to help anyone by being weaker than they are. Do you understand? Do you? Damn it! Do you?"

He was standing up. Shaking his finger violently at the poor seated man. Brother Connors was staring with eyes wide. His lips were quivering. His gaze bright with moisture.

"No. No. You are right, Bishop. No. I see that. I've acted contrary to what I know. I'm very sorry. Very sorry. I'll change. Thank you, Bishop. Thank you."

And with that he was gone.

Brother Connors did not come to sacrament meeting. Bishop Klaus drove over to his house. He knocked for several minutes but no one answered the door. He thought he heard movement.

Bishop Klaus sat through the remainder of that afternoon's meetings with both a hollow anxiety and sinking numbness. He knew he had not been yelling at Brother Connors. He had let his own lust be the catalyst for his anger—at himself. He felt damned. He felt the weight of his failures. And even here. Now. In the midst of his sorrow, the image of Sister Wray in her sweats popped into his head. He was a worm. He tried to clear his thoughts, but as he did so he felt the sinking feeling that heaven was right. He too would fall.

It is pouring rain by the time he locks up the building. A sudden drenching summer storm. He looks up and sighs. He had planned to walk home, but not in the rain. He starts out with a quick pace, but soon he slows. He doesn't even try to cover his head. This feels deserved. He is a wretch. Rather than strengthening weak knees today, he had battered them with a cudgel. He would ask to be released. He would explain to the stake president that he was unworthy. That he could not control his thoughts. Nor his tongue. He was damned and he knew it.

A car suddenly pulls up beside him and a window quickly rolls down. Sister Dillard looks out at him in dismay.

"Bishop Klaus, what are you doing? You're soaked through and through. Please! Can I give you a ride?"

He knows he should not. A brother and sister in the gospel should never be in a car together alone if they are not married to each other. He also knows that nothing matters anymore. He is lost. This is the final straw. He walks over to the passenger door. Gets in the car. Awaits his fate.

He knows Sister Dillard well. Her second marriage had been a disaster. Her husband had been abusive, wielding his priesthood like a weapon, scarring her emotionally and physically. She had come to him often for help. He had talked to the stake president about her husband, suggesting that they bring Sister Dillard's husband to a bishop's court, but the stake president had been disinclined to act, suggesting that maybe she just needed to show an increase of love. He knew the stake president had business dealings with the man. This whole thing had stuck in his craw. When Sister Dillard had said she was leaving her husband, he could not help but rejoice. The man seemed evil. But no one suspected he was a monster because he acted like one of the stalwart.

That was a year ago. During all that time together, he had had a bit of a crush on Sister Dillard. He did not resist the word 'crush' as it played though his mind—as he had before when he was trying to help her. Might as well call things what they were.

So this is how it would end.

They drive in silence awhile. He lifts his eyes up to see her sitting hunched behind the steering wheel, trying to see out of the slightly fogged windshield, the rain hitting the glass in sheets. She wears a simple purple dress with white borders. A gold chain hangs around her neck, the locket resting on her chest. He knows it contains a picture of her sister who died of cancer three years ago. She is a pretty woman. Though not beautiful in a worldly sense, he had always found her fetching.

"My goodness, Bishop, you are going to catch your death of cold in this storm. What were you thinking?" She smiles at him. Her radiance fills the car. His mind begins to wander down all too familiar paths . . .

Then he notices something. Something he'd never seen in her before—she seems happy. He had known her during some of the worst times a person could go through. She had always seemed so emotionally beat-up. So tired. So worn. She now seems . . . it is hard to put a word on it . . . animated? Buoyant? Bright? Content?

"How are you doing these days, Sister Dillard? I've seen you at church, of course, but . . ."

She beams at him. "Better than ever. I'm working at the hospital. I love the people I work for. I'm doing OK."

He nods. "I'm glad to hear it."

She looks over at him and her lips tighten. She blinks a couple of times and then says—almost whispering, staring at the rain pounding the windshield—"You saved my life, Bishop. If you hadn't been there . . ."

He reaches over and puts his hand on her shoulder. She rests her cheek on it.

"I mean there were times I just wanted to die . . . not take my life . . . I would never leave the kids . . . but I just wanted God to bury me in the earth and let blackness take me . . . you were always there."

She laughs, shaking her head. "Anyway. Thank you."

He nods, smiling, and takes his hand away. "I'm so glad you are out of that. So glad."

There is a long comfortable pause. Both remembering what they had been through together.

"Holy cow, Bishop, the canal has flooded over again. I'm going to have to cut around over to Maple to get you home. It's lucky I picked you up."

"That's fine. So are you coming from the single adult 'Linger-Longer'?"

She smiled at that. "Yeah. I love and hate those things."

He laughs.

"I've been seeing someone."

"Really? Who is it?"

"Stan Wilks."

"In the Fourth Ward?"

"Third."

"Excellent. I see him at the stake farm sometimes. Seems a good fellow."

"I'm taking it slow though."

"Good idea."

They both laugh.

Bishop Klaus looks over at Sister Dillard and sees her in depth. He knows her. He knows much about her that few will ever know, and in the complexity of that knowing he knows he could never use her in a way that would spoil their relationship.

She catches him staring at her and says, "You OK?"

He smiles. "Yes. And you are OK, too. I can tell."

As they end-run the flooded canal, they chat about kids, the weather, and a movie they both liked. He feels safe.

She pulls into his driveway.

"Thanks for the ride!" He says brightly.

"It was the least I could do."

He walks up to his doorway and the words that have dogged him the last few weeks appear in his head, "You too shall fall!" But they seem weak and diminished. More an echo.

"Pfffft," he says to the voice, rolling his eyes upward. And he walks into the door determined to get a hold of Brother Connors.

Two-dog Dose

JARRING BANG. WHEELS LEAP UP, RATTLING THE heavy load of black piping destined for the oil rig. The truck rolls on. Oblivious to what it left behind.

On the macadam, a coyote. From its sacrum back to its hips its hindquarters are now flat, pressed hard against the pavement. Its pelvis and thighs pulverized under the weight of the semi. The creature tries to pull itself forward on its front legs. It makes little progress.

The spring air is cold. It is late and stars command a moonless sky. No car passes on this lonesome stretch of road that runs parallel to the Colorado from Highway 191 to the Potash mine, until Lorin Gambel pulls up on the coyote in his '94 Toyota. He shines his headlights onto the beast and sees it making an effort to move, straining against its dead back end, but its exertions fail.

Lorin gets out of the truck and walks toward the coyote. That stirs it into action and it raises itself unto its front legs, snarling viciously. Foam and blood leak from between its teeth. Its eyes, vicious in hatred and rage, flash red in the headlights as it struggles to pull itself forward, warning with its snapping jaws that it is not yet dead. It intends damage.

Lorin hears a clatter from the truck. Avek. An old and distinguished lab climbs from the cab. Slowly. Its grizzled muzzle shows white in the back-splash of the headlights. It stands back from the commotion, hair stiff and standing along her dorsal ridge. She is giving a low rumble at the sight of her raging relative smashed bloodily into the road.

"Avek. Truck!"

Still growling low, the dog obeys. Not reluctantly. Age learns its limits.

The dog's human companion too is feeling the years press and he stares for a time, watching the rage and vitriol of the doomed animal. He walks back to the truck and digs under the driver's seat, through the old pop cans, candy wrappers, and other flotsam to find the holstered .375 Smith & Wesson. It's been sequestered for a long time, yet loaded and ready for use. It feels heavy in his hand. He unholsters the gun and pops the cylinder loose and gives it a spin and sees the ends of the bullets displaying their waiting silver primer. He then locks the cylinder in place and steps away from the car.

The old dog has not watched any of this: her eyes have exclusively focused through the front windshield on the coyote. Her attention has not wavered for even a second.

The unlucky animal has lain back down during this interlude.

Lorin approaches the wounded mess in the road and the coyote rises again onto its front legs. Its vicious rebuke is no less vigorous than before, but there is a tremor in its legs that suggests its time in this world may not be much longer. Lorin gets as close as he dares and takes aim. The savage creature is snarling and biting the air. The pistol fires and the canyon lights up from the muzzle flash like the burst from a lightning strike. Just as he pulls the trigger, however, the coyote snaps its head away and the shot strikes the beast in the muzzle. It is jerking wildly on the ground, shaking its head, trying to dislodge teeth and bone that have shattered loose inside its snout.

"Shit," he says and steps forward, takes a better aim at the skull and fires. There is a bang and a whimper, like both scenarios for the end of the world, followed by stillness—save for the ringing in his ears from the explosion. He hears Avek give an approving bark.

He grabs the coyote by one of its front legs and swings it to the side of the road with enough force that it rolls down the embankment a bit. He then goes back to the truck, takes the leather holster off of the front seat, holsters the gun and slides it back under the seat, pushing the garbage collected there out of the way. He crawls into the seat and gives Avek's head a rub. Then, grabbing the steering wheel, he looks at the large bloodstain on the road. He stares long enough that Avek fidgets with concern and begins to lick his face. He looks at Avek. His eyes well with tears. He starts to cry. His cry is not restrained; he weeps in anguish and sorrow. Sobbing, he accepts the licks of his companion, but finds neither solace or discontentment in the wet tongue that scours his face—for his thoughts are far away. Today he not only killed the coyote, but murdered his best friend Karl Tillman and he was coming out of the canyon to call the sheriff and tell Kay Tillman that her husband was dead.

It happened on this wise.

When he arrived at the Moab hospital he found Kay sitting in the little waiting area. *Wheel of Fortune* was airing silently above her on a thick-backed TV mounted in the corner. She was on a cell phone. She said, "I've got to go. I'll fill you in later."

She hung up the phone as he approached and they wrapped their arms around each other in a tight hug. She kissed him on the cheek and held onto both his hands as they separated. She was wearing jeans, cowboy boots, and a T-shirt. She had a large turquoise necklace and matching earrings. Her hair was in a tight ponytail, gray, with pure white streaking through much of it. They had known each other a long time and he could tell she was worn. Exhausted. Not just from what had happened this morning. It had taken him three hours to drive down from Spanish Fork. He had only stopped to drop off his dog at an old friend's place. After, he came straight here.

"How is he?"

Kay dropped his hands and ran both hands over her head as if trying to press things back into place. She sighed and looked at a nearby door.

"They are stitching him up now. It's a bad gash across his shin. I couldn't watch. Had a devil of a time picking the gravel out."

"Dislocated his shoulder, you said on the phone?"

"Yeah, they set it. The bastard could have killed himself. He's been so lucid since they slapped the Mematorex Patch on him, I'd started thinking he was back to normal."

"Can I see him?"

"Yeah, just go in. He may or may not recognize you. He didn't know me when I got here. They found him out in the golf course. Now he seems perfectly normal. Surprised he is in the hospital, yeah, but he knows me and Doc Pritchett now."

"Ok."

She took his hands again and whispered, "Thanks for coming."

In answer he gave her another big hug and whispered, "Of course."

He walked into the room. Karl was sitting on a white-papered physician's table in a hospital gown. He had one arm in a sling and a doctor was putting a bandage on his lower leg. It looked like he was just finishing.

"You tipped over a golf cart? Really, Karl? That's just lame. If I come all the way down, I expect something dramatic. Something with style, a little panache. At least something like getting bucked off a horse, or wiping out jumping a motorcycle. But a golf cart? You are an embarrassment to old geezers everywhere."

"Damn it. I told that biddy not to call you. I'm fine." But his eyes betrayed him. He was glad Lorin had come. It was obvious he was afraid.

Lorin crossed the room and tried to give him a hug but it became more of a friendly pat as he tried to avoid the wounded shoulder and the bandaged leg.

"So what happened?"

Karl looked down.

He was clearly avoiding the conversation so Lorin dropped it. "Are they going to let you go?"

"Yeah, they want to up the meds." He looked down as the doctor gave him some instructions and then left the room for a minute. He looked up at his friend. "It's getting bad. I don't know where I am sometimes. I'll just sit still for awhile and it will usually come back, but it's taking longer and today apparently I never came back."

"Maybe they just need to adjust the meds like you said."

"Last week in Salt Lake the brain doctor said the granules are starting to show up more and more—" There was a long pause, then, "It's going to go bad."

"How's Kay taking it?"

"Not good. She's worn out from worrying. She's been reading up on it and she is getting more and more depressed. I picked up one of the books and . . ." he paused again, "and the next few years are going to be hell."

Lorin knew he was right. He had watched his brother's wife go down with it and it took five years to take her all the way under, but in most ways she was gone in three. The lights were on, but no one was home. Thank goodness his wife had gone quickly five years ago. A heart attack that slowed her down, then another that had taken her in her sleep. He thought about what the next years of Kay's life would be. He looked at the wall.

"Well, I'm going to help as I can. I can get down here a little more. I've been thinking of retiring from the university anyway."

"Well, you'll help me now. It's time."

Lorin understood instantly. "No! It's too early."

"Look, we agreed. It's my call. You can't break the pact now."

"It's too early."

"This ain't going nowhere but down. Right now my kids have great memories of me. Kay is still strong and chances are she has got some good years with the grandkids coming. After five years of watching me Titanic she'll be a shell. Already it's killing her. I can see it. I invoke the pact. My call."

"No."

"Don't do this. We've talked about it for fifteen years. We swore on the hunt. My call. I invoke the pact."

Lorin looked at his friend. He knew he was right. But he always thought he'd go first. This was something Karl was going to do for him. Not vice versa.

"Look, Karl. It's crazy. We'll both end up in the Terrestrial Kingdom."

Karl laughed. "You haven't believed in that for years. I'm the religious one. Remember? And I think the Lord is OK with this. This is an act of courage. Jesus laid down his life. I'm just following him."

"Karl, I'm not going to kill you."

"Yes, you are. I invoke the pact."

That night after dinner, they were sitting out on the deck looking at the glow of the La Sals in the setting sun. Their bellies were full of good T-bone steak that Karl cooked one-handed. Old-style over charcoals. Kay had conjured up a potato salad and some camp beans, flavored with the same sauce the beef was marinated in. They were drinking Postum mixed with hot chocolate, Karl's invention nearly twenty-five years ago on a deer hunt. He called it Nephi's savory coffee, then it became just NSC. It had been a staple until the company quit making Postum years ago, and he had brought it back when they started making it again.

To Lorin the flavor brought back memories—delicious with bright colors. He and Karl had been friends since they roomed together at BYU and as he looked at his old friend he felt a loss that hung over him like the sword of Damocles. He could *not* kill him as he wanted. Yet he could not *not* honor the pact. It had been a sacred part of many a Canyonlands hike. He knew what lay ahead for his friend and his wife and his eyes welled with tears as he thought about the darkness just over the horizon.

The tops of the La Sals were bathed in orange light and the desert rock that lay before them had almost disappeared in darkness. The three old friends were silent as they watched the last of the sunlight climb toward the summit of Tuk, Utah's third highest mountain. Lorin sighed. There were things he could do. And things he could not. Despite his promises he would not kill him.

He looked at Karl. Karl was staring back at him strangely. A mixture of fear and, what? Karl turned to Kay with that same expression. She looked at him at that moment and fear stamped her face with such immediacy Lorin took in a breath.

"Karl? Are you OK?" There was panic in her voice.

He was looking at Lorin, then at Kay. His face was a mask of confusion and fear. His eyes were wide. He stood up.

"Excuse me. Who are you? Are you from the church? From the stake?"

"Karl. It's me Lorin. Remember? We were just talking about the deer hunt."

He sat down cowed but his obvious fear and confusion did not abate.

Kay said, "Karl. It's me. Kay. Remember?"

He gave a very fake smile, "Kay. Yes. Of course. I remember we've met. I'm Karl."

Kay was crying now, she jumped up and ran into the house, tears streaming down her face.

Karl continued his fake smile. "Did I say something to upset her? Do I know you?"

He could see Kay in the kitchen pacing frantically and talking to someone on the phone.

"Excuse me a minute, Karl." Lorin ran into the kitchen. "Are you OK?"

"Don't leave him alone!" she screamed and sure enough when he

got back he was gone, but he had not gone far. He was standing at
the side of the house, confused.

Karl looked at his friend and said, "I'm sorry, but I can't remember where I live. Can you take me home? I think the house is yellow."

"You live here, Karl. This is your house."

"This isn't my house."

The fear in his face was turning to anger. "Please take me home,
or leave me alone."

"Karl, this is your house."

"This is isn't my house!" he yelled. "Get away from me!"

Kay was running toward him waving her arms. "Don't make him
angry," she whispered.

"Can someone tell me where I am? Where do I live?"

"Karl, just relax, this will pass. You'll remember." He walked
toward him, holding out his hands in a gesture of reconciliation.

"Stay away from me!"

"Karl." He then reached out to reassure his friend. His friend
punched him hard in the face. Lorin went down. His nose broken.
Kay screamed. Karl ran.

Lorin got up quickly. His nose was bleeding, but he took off
after Karl. Just then an ambulance pulled up and Kay ran over
and directed it toward the man running down the gravel lane that
fronted the house.

The ambulance driver was a young kid who had been nearby
when he got the call. He ran to Karl quickly, but it did not go well.
The driver grabbed Karl and Karl went crazy, swinging wildly. The
kid, obviously not trained to handle this, blew up in anger and a
full-blown fight erupted. Kay ran over and tried to pull the driver
off her husband. He had fallen and the driver was trying to sit on
him to hold him down. Karl found an old piece of rebar and swung
out hard from his supine position and capped the knee of the
driver. The sound of the crack pushed Lorin out of his shock and
he ran over and pulled the kid away from Karl who was snarling

like a cornered animal. Kay was hysterical. The police arrived. The kid was rolling on the ground clutching his knee. Kay was beating the officer's chest with her fists begging him to help her husband. Two more officers arrived. Karl had to be cuffed and was placed in the back of the police car. Kay was placed in the second ambulance, clutching one hand with her other. Somehow in the scuffle and confusion she had broken two fingers. The kid from the ambulance was put in a stretcher and loaded onto a third ambulance, which tore away with the siren and the kid screaming.

Lorin tried to explain to one of the officers what had happened while holding some ice to his nose. Was it really only thirty minutes ago that they had been watching the rays of the sunset igniting the La Sals?

Two days later Karl was sitting on the couch watching TV. His eyes were glazed and somewhat blank. He knew where he was. He knew who Lorin was. He knew he was in his own house. But he was drugged. Sedated. Just until his new meds had time to adjust things, the doctor said. No one could risk another episode like the one from the other day. Best to ensure his calmness chemically.

Lorin was sitting at the kitchen table across from Kay. Her eyes were red and swollen; the bags under her eyes aged her ten years. She hugged a large convenience store Diet Coke. She looked at Lorin and tried to say something, but just looked past him to her husband. Finally she said, "I can't do this."

"Kay, this is temporary. The doctor said he just needs to get his medicine stable and . . ."

Kay was looking at him like he was an imbecile. She smiled sadly at him. "It will never get better. Only worse and worse and worse and worse . . ." She trailed off into a sob.

He got up and put his arm around her. She did not move to return his embrace. He looked at his friend and the sad empty look on his face. Eyes hollow.

He felt Kay's sobs along his arm wrapped around her back. *Worse and worse and worse,* she had said.

Karl had invoked the pact.

"It *will* be all right," he said to Kay, stroking her head and staring at Karl.

Lorin watched as Kay leaned into the window and kissed Karl good-bye. She said she was pleased to have a couple of days to get some things done. The last few weeks had been a mixture of bad and good. Sometimes he was as cogent as he was right now. Occasionally he faded, but the sedation kept him from acting up. Lorin had driven down again from Spanish Fork, ostensibly to give Kay a break.

"We'll be fine. We are going to the temple, walk the grounds, maybe ask someone to add a few names to the prayer roll—don't worry, I won't let him go in by himself. It's the House of the Lord. This is a good thing. Then we'll explore some of our old stomping grounds and maybe jog his memory circuits a little."

She nodded. Kissed Karl and stepped away from the car. She looked worried. Lorin had talked her out of giving Karl the drugs that kept him calm. She had believed him when he said that he would be blessed for visiting the newly built temple in Monticello. Karl assured her that he would be fine.

They pulled away and she watched until they turned onto the highway toward Monticello about fifty miles south of Moab. As she passed out of sight, Lorin turned left onto a side road. She would not see them as they turned away from the city driving south and then doubled back north on Spanish Valley Drive, back onto the highway, and back through town. Most of the way both men were silent. After passing the Arches National Park entrance, they turned west on Potash Road.

"You all right?" Karl asked as they began following the Colorado toward the potash mine.

"No."

"I suspect not. But you're doing the right thing."

Lorin did not answer. He looked at his friend. "Just stay with me. OK. Try hard."

"I'll do my best."

They found the old jeep trail they were looking for and turned up it. It took considerable skill to maneuver over the old mining road. Avek, lying on the back bench, kept being tossed to the floor. She finally gave up repeatedly climbing back onto the backseat and just stayed on the footrests.

"She's a good dog," Karl said.

"That she is. I was so mad when Sandy brought her home after the kids left. But she's been one damn good dog. She's seen me through a lot."

"Get Kay a dog. OK? A good one. A lab like Avek."

"Shit, to replace you? I'll get her a city pound mutt. That seems more appropriate."

"Take care of her."

"Take care of her? Hell, I'm going to sweep her off her feet and talk her into marrying me. Steal her right out from under your nose and when she gets to heaven she'll be saying, 'I want Lorin.'"

Lorin was surprised to find he was crying, making his claims lose some of their force.

Karl smiled. "It won't work. I see what you're doing. Trying to get me to stick around. Forget the pact. Nope. I wouldn't mind you taking Kay. They say in heaven everything will get sorted out. And besides," Karl laughed, "you don't believe in the Celestial Kingdom no more so you'll get nothing on the other side. Likely they'll castrate the likes of you. So have fun with Kay, she'll be your last taste of a woman for next zillion years."

Karl was now crying too.

They went through a rough patch where some of the road had washed away, creating a bit of tricky maneuvering. It looked for a moment like Lorin was going to leave them high centered, but he pulled it off.

"Hey. Be careful coming back. I don't want to see you on the other side for a few years at least."

"Whatever."

They went on climbing along the edge of a high ridge.

"Can you imagine the work it took to cut this road?" Karl observed.

"This is the kind of stuff my dad did."

"Really? He must have been disappointed his son became an English professor."

"Yeah. I think he was, actually. Maybe. Hard to say. He was a difficult man to read. Sometimes I thought he was as proud as hell about me, other times I wondered if he thought my life had been wasted."

Karl suddenly said, "Pull over." He seemed scared and Lorin worried that he might have started slipping away, but his friend added, "I want to change into my temple clothes."

"You know they are just going to rot."

"Well, no one knows the day or time of His appearance. I want to be buried properly. I wish you could dedicate my grave, but given your heathen status . . ."

The truck stopped. Both Karl and Lorin got out of the car and he let Avek out to give her a chance to stretch her legs a bit. Karl changed into his white clothes, and put on the accouterments of a man garbed in the robes of the High Priesthood, like someone ready to make temple covenants, or to meet the Lord should the need arise.

Lorin pulled some sandwiches out of a bag and passed one to Karl decked out in his priestly garb. He pulled a couple of Mountain Dews out of a little cooler and handed one to his friend. They ate in silence after a brief toast to Kay for providing such a perfect lunch and a couple of teases that the food was reason enough for Lorin to go after Kay when Karl was gone.

But after a couple of bites Lorin set the sandwich down. His appetite fled so he gave the sandwich to Avek. Karl ate with relish, savoring each bite with a look of contentment on his face. After eating without a word they got back in the truck and continued banging up the unruly mining road.

Lorin looked over at Karl. "You know you look ridiculous in that getup."

"I remember the first time I put it on. It was all supposed to be sacred, but when I saw everyone dressed like this, I couldn't help but laugh. So there I was in the temple, knee deep in what was supposed to be the most holy experience of my life and I can't help it but I'm trying damn hard to suppress my giggles."

Lorin, focusing on the road, said, "Not me. I took it so serious I felt like I was standing before God Himself. There was an aura over everything. I felt like every electron in my body had suddenly reversed directions because everything had changed in fundamental ways. Everything was new."

"Ironic, hey, how you are now the unbeliever and me who laughed at the sacred am hanging on until . . ."

"Funny. Yeah. Maybe I took it so earnestly I broke it. It couldn't stand the gravity of my seriousness and it just collapsed. Maybe if I would have laughed more at it, I could have found something to cling to."

"Maybe it's not too late."

"Maybe."

A few hundred yards from their destination a rockslide blocked the road with red rock boulders ranging in size from basketballs to Volkswagens.

"Looks like we are going to have to walk," Karl said brightly. There was a giddiness about him as if he were a kid about to sit on Santa's lap.

"I reckon so."

Lorin took a small backpack out of the back of the truck and grabbed a shovel strapped to the side of the bed and threw it across his shoulder. He took a large bolt cutter out of a box in the back and handed it to Karl saying, "Here, you carry the heavy stuff."

They easily skirted the slide and started their march to the mine-shaft. Karl in his temple slippers was walking carefully, almost mincing toward their destination. His robe blew in the slight wind and he had to hold down his cap to keep the occasional gust from unsettling it.

"What's the shovel for?"

"Clean up the dog poop. Can't leave a mess in the wilderness," Lorin joked, giving both men a laugh, but then he added, "I don't know exactly. Just thought I'd bring it. Who knows, maybe I'll need to hit you in the head with it if you don't go down easily."

"Just don't mess up my beautiful face."

The men moved slowly. The old, slightly arthritic dog followed closely behind, seeming content with the easy pace. They moved now in silence. There was a strong sense of belonging here. The sage and juniper, the red rock, the scattered pieces of yellowcake, the blue-bellied lizards darting away as they approached. It was all intimately familiar. They knew this land. They had both been raised in Moab and had spent a lifetime wandering its environs.

There was a wide clearing in front of the mine. They found a large flat rock and they both sat down on it. Sweating and puffing. A palpable fear starting to grace both their faces. They both looked at the big gate bolted deep into the rock over the entrance.

"Bats," Karl said.

"What?"

"Bats. That's why the BLM put these gates in. It turns out these mines are critical bat nurseries. If people come around disturbing the bats, entire generations might be lost."

"OK. Bats."

Karl walked over to the chained door with the bolt cutter. It was secured with a thick chain.

"Lorin! A little help here."

Lorin got up and between the two of them squeezing the huge calipers, the bolt came free. They opened the gate and wandered about thirty yards in until they came to a large hole that shot straight down. They both looked into the shaft.

"Deep."

"Yeah. About a hundred feet, if our plumb line was right when we were here twenty years ago."

"Twenty years ago."

"Yup."

They walked back out of the mine and sat down on the same rock. Finally Lorin said, "I don't want to do this."

"We made a pact. I'm holding you to it."

Lorin looked at him for a long time. The face he had known longer than any living soul. "What if next year they discover a drug that will make it all better?"

"If wishes were fishes we'd all have a fry. Let's do this. The longer we wait the harder it will be. Let's get it over with."

Lorin did not move for a long time. Finally he fished a couple of small bottles out of his daypack.

"I told Avek's vet that he was too old and it was time to put him down. I told him I had a lady friend whose German shepherd was ready to go too and we were going to the mountains to do it together. I've known the vet all Avek's life and he was good enough to give me both doses."

"I'm getting a two-dog dose then."

"Yup," he said, then hesitantly held out bottles. "It's your call. If you use them, this is you not me."

Karl did not take them.

"What happens?"

"The vet said that it takes about twenty minutes before the dog falls asleep. Once asleep he'll last about ten more. Then he sleeps forever."

Karl nodded and reached for the pills. "OK then. For Kay."

"For Kay."

Lorin sighed and handed him the pills. "There's five in each bottle, take them all."

"Any side effects?" Karl asked. Both men burst into laughter.

"Not if used as directed." Lorin smirked.

"Consult your doctor to make sure your heart is healthy enough for death," Karl joked, but it fell flat.

Lorin just said, "Yeah."

Karl took a water bottle out of his pack, poured all the pills into his hand, and swallowed them down in almost one gulp. He finished and said, "That's that."

The men sat in silence for a few minutes looking over the landscape.

"Lorin?"

"Yeah."

"Thanks."

"It was a pact. I swore an oath. Thank that. I'm not happy about this."

"Kay will be. Not if you told her. Not if she suspected anything. It will sting at first, but in a year from now she'll start moving on. Being a grandma. She'll get over it. Otherwise, in a year she'd be hollowed out and empty from taking care of me. She'll have worried herself into a short life."

"I suppose."

"The kids will remember me strong. With a good mind. No memories of a blank deer-eyed man staring at nothing and who has no idea who he is. Are you going to stick to the plan?"

"Yeah. I'll drive down to Bluff and that footpath that crosses the San Juan by the reservation. I'll say we were remembering good times and I turned around when I heard a big splash."

"Tell her we didn't call from Monticello because we were having so much fun."

"I'll tell her. Don't worry."

"And we drove to Bluff to remember more good times. She'll understand the need to visit memories with this thing I've got looming."

"I'll tell her."

"And you'll call the police."

"Yup."

"They'll drag the river."

"Yeah."

"It's running high with the thaw. No one will even expect to find my body."

"I suppose."

"Lorin?"

"Yeah?"

"Thanks for doing this. It's right. It's going to fix a lot of things that would get broken."

"I think you are very brave. This will be a good death."

Lorin reached out and put his arm around Karl who leaned into him. They were silent a while.

Karl pulled back and looked at him. "Sir, you are a good friend!" His voice sounded somewhat slurred. Lorin knew the medicine was taking effect.

"Karl, you are a good friend too. I love you, buddy."

"I love you too, but let's not muddy this up getting sappy."

They were silent a few more minutes. Then Karl said in a very slurred voice, "Last night I didn't know where I was. I was laying on my bed and I did not know where in the hell I was. I thought I must be staying in a hotel somewhere. I saw Kay beside me and I thought my hell who am I in bed with. It was strange. I thought I'd just lie there until things came back to me. I fell asleep."

"I'm glad you were awake today."

"Me too."

"Lorin, I'm tired. Can I just lay down here in the sand? Just for a minute."

Lorin helped him from the rock and assisted him so he could lay down on his back. He opened his eyes for a while looking at the one lone cloud in the sky.

"I love this place. I love the desert. I love you. I love Kay. I love God."

"They all love you, too."

Karl closed his eyes and began to breathe more evenly.

"Karl?"

"Umm?"

"Let me know what's on the other side."

"Ummmmmmbb."

Karl slept for some time. Longer than the ten minutes that the vet suggested. His breathing got shallower and shallower and several times Lorin checked to see if he was breathing. He repeatedly was. After about fifteen minutes he worried something had gone wrong. After twenty-five minutes Karl made a funny sound, raspy and hollow. It was his last breath.

It was getting late in the afternoon. Lorin wept for a bit. He watched the body of his friend until flies started to gather and land on the corpse. He decided to get to work. He had never intended to throw his body into the mine. He knew he could not stand the sound of his friend's body striking the bottom of the shaft. He also worried that some kids would invariably break into the mine and do something crazy like rappel down the shaft. They would discover the body. That would raise questions and likely start an investigation. Karl had always had more faith in gates and locks than he had.

He walked over and picked up the shovel and walked down to a rock overhang a good sixty feet down and west of the mine. A rock overhang—part of a larger red rock formation—created a depression that protected what was once a small sandstone bowl that had, over the centuries, filled with sand. Over the top was a patchwork crusting of cryptobiotic matting, the delicate microbial mass that stabilized much of this desert soil, giving the sandy surface the crumbly look of an overdone coffee cake. This he delicately removed by digging beneath it and placing it carefully a few feet away. Once the sand was exposed, digging was easy. Still it took most of the remaining afternoon to get a hole about four feet around. He dug until he hit sandstone, likely the lower portion of the tipped over bowl that shaped the overhang. The configuration of rock allowed the wind to slowly fill up the bowl with the sand he had just removed; if he left it for a century or so it would fill back up. A friend of his called these formations wind-blown sand eddies.

He climbed back up to the mine and tied a bit of rope around Karl's legs and dragged him carefully down the hill. Once he could have carried him, but now it took everything just to drag him downhill to his grave. Avek was very curious about Karl and kept sniffing him and looking inquiringly at Lorin for some explanation.

He dragged him right into the hole, but his body was left sort of sitting up and leaning on his side against one of the walls of the grave. Lorin jumped down and arranged him on the floor of the hole, on his side and slightly curled up. He climbed out of the grave and rested a while.

He looked at the grave with Karl resting in his dirty and disheveled temple clothes. His cap had fallen off and his apron and robe were twisted all round. This would not do. Although he was no longer a believer he believed in Karl and his intent. He jumped into the grave and brushed the sand off of his clothes and arranged them properly as was fitting a High Priest of the Lord. When all was done he climbed back out of the hole and stood by the side of the grave. He felt like he should say something and remembered back to when he was a bishop in the Church. He had dedicated many graves and he decided that despite his heathen status Karl deserved a proper Mormon ritual.

In the low, late afternoon sun he looked around him. While he no longer believed in the white bearded god he had grown up with, there was something powerful in the landscape that lay all around him. A presence that made itself felt. An ancient attendance that cared very little about him, but that he could acknowledge and feel. An old god. This was something he could worship. So while the rituals that had shaped the people of this landscape had been born elsewhere, they had entered this land and made themselves part of the high desert, the wind and water carved variegated Canyonlands. He was a part of the landscape and the people that called it home. He knew what to do.

He raised his arm to a square pointing his palm toward the rusty reds, oranges, and white sandstones in the valley below:

By the power of the Holy Melchizedek Priesthood I hold, I dedicate this grave to be the final resting place of my friend Karl Tillman. I ask that this place be hallowed ground and will be protected from the elements and beasts that would disturb this place, until the morning of the First Resurrection. In which you will arise Karl, if anyone will.

Then he sensed that strange force which had always overcome him whenever he had given priesthood blessings to his wife, or children while they were growing up. He felt his voice detach from his own will and speak as power flowed from something higher and better than he was.

I bless you Karl that you'll not be found here. I bless your children that they will find comfort in the goodness of your life. That the things you taught them as a father will be remembered and cherished. That your life will be recalled as worthy of emulation. I bless that Kay will be comforted by the Holy Ghost and she will also find meaning in your life and will remember and hold onto those memories that you both cherish. Karl, I bless your friend who took your life that he will forgive himself for what he's done and take comfort in the sacrifice you have made for your family. God bless you Karl wherever you are.

I say these things in the sacred name of Jesus Christ. Amen.

Lorin started to shake and sob as he picked back up the shovel and with blurry eyes filled in the grave. When it was about half full he carried and rolled some large flat stones to form a protective barrier from predators that might sense something aging under the sand. It was nearly dark when he finished burying the flagstones he had placed over his friend. When he was done, as carefully as he could, he replaced the soil surface crust. It didn't work as well as he hoped, much of it crumbling as he tried to place it, but it was something that gave it an air of having never been disturbed. Mostly.

On the wall of the overhang where the stone entered the sand that made up the grave, he carved with his pocket knife, "Karl

Tillman, 2014." It would be mistaken for a random bit of graffiti, if anyone ever noticed it, such as is common to the rock faces and aspens of this area. He walked back to the gate on the mine and tried to fix the chain they had cut. He put the links together and angled them in a way that would hold together unless someone noticed the cut and reoriented them to loose the links. He pulled the chain in a way that the break was hidden behind the gate.

It was done. Karl was dead. Murdered really. But he felt so light he started to sing one of the old hymns of his youth through his tears.

There is blood on his hands. There is also blood all over his pants and shirt. Why had he not noticed what the coyote had left on him? It will not do to call the Bluff sheriff covered in blood and claim his friend has gone missing. He walks down to the Colorado and washes his hands in the very cold, brown, sandy water. He's near a sandbar and wades out through calf-deep water and takes his shirt off and washes it quickly like his pioneer ancestors might have. He keeps his trousers on, but takes up a handful of river sand and scrubs his pants clean with it. The blood is fresh and the water cold and the stains come out easily.

He hikes back up to the truck passing the dead coyote grimacing at him. Its eyes are fixed on nothing and everything. Lorin is exhausted. He spreads his shirt onto the back seat, places his shoes on the floor of the backbench, and then climbs into the driver's seat. He reaches over and scratches Avek's head. She seems jittery and eagerly licks his hand.

"It's been quite a day, girl. Still some shit to do."

He then puts the truck in gear and pulls away. Leaving behind the coyote on the side of the road.

The Best Pinewood Derby Ever

SOME FOLK REMEMBER IT AS THE YEAR THE BISHOP of the Pleasant Grove 2nd Ward went mad. But it was a delightful insanity and created one of my favorite childhood memories. It was pinewood derby time. The whole ward took this very seriously. Very seriously indeed. Every year the boys were supposed to get their official pinewood derby kit and with minimal help from their parents have a fun race down the track amid the cheers of all the participants. But it was never like that. Parents *were* involved and every year a black market for derby secrets would emerge with some people, like the Hilliards and the Wilds, spending hundreds of dollars on winning designs from the pinewood derby underground. This was before the Internet, so finding those who would sell their secrets was sometimes tricky. But if you got desperate, you could always find pinewood derby designs among the ads found in the *Pleasant Grove Soldier of Fortune Monthly* or in *The Feel'n Grovy Beat* and other rags of ill repute.

That year the bishop was fed up with telling the parents to let the boys do their own work and no one listening, so at the big meeting where the kits were distributed the bishop stood up and said, "This year we are going to do things differently." A hush fell over the crowd. The painfully rich Wilds had a scowl, and their eyebrows were raised to the top of their foreheads, because you can bet they had been on the prowl for some hidden knowledge and maybe had even gotten

151

involved with the local mafia or those who practice black magic to obtain it, and so were not going to take any "new" regulations kindly.

The bishop looked over the crowd and said, "This year there are no rules. Do anything you want." After a moment of stunned silence, a zillion hands went up, all asking for clarification. But the bishop kept repeating, no rules. Can parents help their kids? No rules. Are there weight restrictions? No rules. Do you have to use the wheels in the kit? No rules. Does it have to stay on the track the whole time? Yes. One rule. That. On and on the questions came until the room was abuzz. Can girls race? No rules. Can people work together? No rules. There were some who were angry at first, but for the most part there was an air of palpable excitement. Parents started whispering with their kids. The room was charged with electricity. Even the Wilds and the Hilliards had a gleam in their eye after a few minutes of red-faced outrage.

The day of the race the track was set up in the gym and shortly after it looked like things were about to go sour. The stake president, a gruff old ex-Marine colonel, had come to see his grand-nephew race a car made of lead that was as heavy as that sounds. When the president saw one of the cars had an Estes A8-3 model rocket engine sticking out he angrily called the bishop over. The bishop said, let's discuss this outside the gym and they walked out together with the SP gesticulating wildly. In a few minutes the bishop came back and when one of his councilors asked where the stake president was, he said cheerily, I've locked him in the utility closet. He'll be mad as hell when we let him out, but what's he going to do? Release me? Well, let's get started!

The ones based only on gravity were eliminated pretty fast. I think everyone was a little sad when Widow Simmons' doily covered pie racer (so called because it was made of baked pie dough) was eliminated, but we all gave a cheer for every one of her 97 years. Those rocket-powered, or that used a small BB-gun CO_2 cylinder, did better, but tended not to stay on the track. Seeing pinewood derby cars flying helter-skelter through the gym was great fun although people diving out of their way and protecting small children tended to create worried looks among the spectators until a few wised-up and got blankets out of their cars under which they would hide whenever a rocket powered car was racing about the gym. Soon the rest caught on and did the same, sometimes sharing a large blanket among those that had none. Of course when a car left the track they were disqualified, because of the one rule, so the later heats were a little less star-spangled-bannery. By this time, though, there were some pretty deep scorch marks on the gym floor.

Well, every time there was a pause in the action for set up, we could all hear the stake president bellowing to be let out, but even though we gave each other knowing glances no one made a move to release him. We really were having fun.

We were all secretly pleased when it turned out that the Wilds and the Hilliards were out early. The Wilds used a rocket engine on an inverted wing sitting on the car to keep it on the track, but they ran against the McNultys' daughter, Sarah-anne, who rigged up a clip of paintballs and a short-barreled airgun to fire as it went down the track. That knocked the Wild's car a good ten feet off the track in the first seconds of their heat, even before their rocket engine had fired. Because of the paintball it took to the side it was still airborne when the engine ignited, and it beelined straight into the basketball standard, cracking it a bit. They complained to the bishop who just looked at them, then shook his head smiling, and said, No rules. The Hilliards' car just plain exploded and we were just glad the track wasn't damaged enough to stop the races, but their car was unsalvageable.

There was a hamster-powered car (not that fast), cars that had wound-up rubber bands powering propellers, cars launched from slingshots, and lots of very heavy cars. Some cars were just good old fashioned street-legal high craftsmanship kit-cars that would have faired well under normal rules, which we all thought were lame until we realized they were the only ones eligible to go on to the regional level races (one of which took fourth!).

Well, the final race was between Sarah-anne (who had literally knocked out the competition) and the Davises who had attached a two-cycle model airplane engine to power thick soft rubber wheels on a modified axle. It was wicked fast. When the lever was pulled the Davises who had seen the take down of many a car by a paintball round did something smart, they reversed the propeller so it held steady in place. Down the track, fairly slowly, went the weaponized car popping out paintballs as it went. Halfway down it was out of ammo. The Davises then turned that airplane engine to full throttle and that car zoomed down the track in a cloud of oily smoke as fast as any rocket-powered car that ran that day. It shot past Sarah-anne's ten feet before the end, taking the cup. The place exploded with cheers, whistles, and hoorahs. Even Sarah-anne who just lost was clapping and smiling like a rodeo queen.

The bishop was released and disfellowshipped for locking up the stake president, which the bishop didn't seem to mind if the truth be told. And the $6000 in damage to the gym and track was covered by an anonymous donor. We suspected it was the Wilds and/ or the Hilliards, which let us forgive them for being rich. All in all, though, it was the best pinewood derby we ever had. And I suspect we ever will have.

The Gift of the King's Jeweler

1

Az could hear his wife trying to coax the embers of last night's cooking fire to life in the next room. His youngest son was trying courageously to help, and his short puffs sounded full of pluck but ineffectual next to his wife's slow, steady, whistle-like blow. Az fell back on his mat, not yet ready to begin the day. His eyes stared at the rough log-pole beams that supported the ceiling, and he tried to reconstruct the baffling dream that had come once again to harass his sleep.

In it, a wheel was spinning, round and round—turning brilliantly in his mind. It was made of beautiful brass, bathed in light, with words and pieces of words flying off the wheel at an indescribable speed. Then a piercing voice cried, "You are called to an odyssey of wonder and light! Forge!" Suddenly, the dream shifted softly, running forward as if Az had been brought over a great journey, across vast distances and over many lifetimes. He had the impression that he had been thrown far into the future in a single breath, which left him only lingering shards of forgotten memories. Then he found himself outside. The night air seemed cool but not cold. It was early springtime; the sky was alight with stars so bright that he realized it must be a dream. But one star—there were no words to describe it—one star shone with such brilliance it was like none he had ever seen, or even imagined. Next to him stood men of stunning wealth and power; perhaps wise counselors of some great king, perhaps great prophets or seekers of wisdom. One turned to him, smiled and asked, "What gift will you bring?"

He always woke up after the voice, with his heart beating and his breast filled with a peace and a lightness that almost left him laughing. These feelings were replaced, however, with a shallow melancholy as he realized that he could not understand what God was trying to tell him; for surely it was God. Who else could have sent a dream so beautiful? But what had it meant?

Az smelled the modest cooking fire almost at the same time he heard its welcoming crackle. That was the signal for the rest of the household to arise. His son-in-law would soon be at the bellows heating the kiln to the temperature Az would need to melt the lumps of metal he would turn into art—gold and silver that would adorn the neck, arms, and legs of the king and his consorts, and others in his favor. His mother would soon be grinding wheat, which his wife would turn into bread. His oldest daughter would help polish the gold amulet he had made yesterday for the king's concubine, while her son—his grandson—played outside in the fields. His youngest daughter would spend the day watching her father, standing a respectable distance away, but never taking her eyes off him as he molded, hammered, and shaped the metals into adornment for royalty. She loved the forge. She loved the smells. She loved watching the glowing metals pulled fiery-hot from the kiln and transformed, as if by magic (by her father's steady, patient hands), into works of staggering beauty and delight. She would watch him as he slowly, and without a wasted move, made chains of gold or silver link by link, sometimes taking weeks. Though her attention was flattering, Az worried about her. She took no interest in the labor that women were supposed to do. Nonetheless, he enjoyed his little "Melon-Flower," as he called her, who seldom left his forge.

The day was beginning. One of the king's guards poked his shaggy head in and asked for a drink of water from Az's mother. She let out a long sigh and slowly meandered to the water urn balancing snugly in the corner.

"Why can't the king send water to quench the thirst of these rabble? I have to carry load after load of water from the well just so these refugees from the army can sit outside my door gambling!"

"Give him the water, Mother! They've worked hard all night keeping you safe from murderers and thieves," Az called out cheerfully from his bed. He was never quite comfortable with guards stationed around his home—a necessary evil for the king's jeweler.

"Safe!" His mother harrumphed. "I've no doubt of that. Their snoring would have kept out Enki himself. Ishtar be praised that we get any sleep in our safety."

The soldier laughed and went outside with the water.

Az stepped from the room where he slept then looked at his mother unhappily.

"Mother. Please don't say that name in my house."

His mother looked at him and spat into the fire. "Ishtar," she said, staring at him. "Ishtar! Ishtar! Ishtar!"

Az shook his head. "Mother, please."

"You come back from your travels with a new god—fine. But don't expect me to fall on my knees before your Hebrew idol. Ishtar has watched over me since I was a little girl. And no god, especially one whose name you don't know, will take her place!"

Az looked at her coldly, then softened. "Mother, you are lucky that the God I worship teaches love and patience. You don't understand. This is not just a new god. It is *the* God. The only one. The one true God who made the heavens and the earth."

"Pshaw!" His mother snorted. "Anu made all that."

"No, mother. It was the One God. I know that because His Spirit has changed me. I am a new person . . ."

"I've no doubt of that. Since your trip south you have become impossible to live with!" She gave an ironic laugh. "And you've taken our enemy's god no less! What would the king do if he knew that, eh?"

"I don't care what the king knows." With that Az threw his hands into the air and walked back into his room. A soft red light came through a hole in the ceiling as the morning sun stretched above the rooftops of Babylon. The sound of a rooster cut through the cool morning air and, almost as punctually, the voice of his neighbor arguing with his two wives rose above the sound of ass hooves clipping their way to market. The tinkling of bells rushing hurriedly past his door confessed that the temple harlots were on their way to Ishtar's shrine. Az thought about his 'new' God. The creator of the earth, the stars, the Euphrates, birds, and even the pig—whose hocks he could no longer enjoy as a worshiper of this Lord of Lords. What a wondrous God this was! Az fell on his knees. He faced Jerusalem to remember the Temple and the place of his conversion and prayed. He prayed for strength to endure his mother's complaints. He prayed for his family. He prayed that there would be no war between Babylon and the southern kingdoms, whose God he had embraced. But mostly he prayed for help in understanding the dream. The dream of the spinning rings, the changing words, and the brightest of stars.

2

THE GUARD LOUDLY INVADED THE FOUNDRY AND stood rigidly in an obvious place until Az looked up from the bracelet he was gently tapping into shape.

"The king's agent is here and wishes to speak to you at once," the guard said officially.

Az sighed in acceptance and said, in a rote voice that belied his words, "Tell him I am glad he honors my humble abode. I will attend him presently."

He picked up the gold bracelet he was fashioning and placed it in a tray that he slid into a cooler part of the kiln to keep it malleable until he returned. He came into the main room of his house wiping his hands on his leather apron. Everyone had gathered in the room to stare silently at the powerful man who had come under their roof.

Even after a year of being the king's jeweler Az still found the presence of such a man intimidating.

"Good day to you. I am the agent of Nebuchadnezzar, Glorious King of Babylon, Worshiper of Marduk, and Builder of the sacred gardens of Nabu. I've come to obtain the amulet for the king's favorite concubine." He then added ominously, "And to be sure the king, our God, is not being cheated."

The king's agent trusted no one, and he treated everyone with intense suspicion. He was powerful, knew it, and acted accordingly—polite conversation abandoned.

Az's oldest daughter brought the gold amulet and handed it quickly to one of the agent's aides. With flair, the eunuch theatrically wrapped it in an elegant purple cloth, then with a deep bow, delivered it to the king's agent. He in turn held it up to the light and inspected it closely. Az's wife held her breath as he turned it over repeatedly, inspecting it closely with his narrow, penetrating eyes. Az did not worry. He knew the quality of his work. He had spent five years in Egypt learning from the greatest metalsmiths in the world. He did not fear this odious man or the king he worshiped as a god.

"The quality will be acceptable to his highness, our God. You are lucky he is patient with weakness."

Az bowed, but said nothing.

"The scales and the touchstone!" One of the agent's aides, another large eunuch, stepped forward, then, drawing items from a series of small leather bags, constructed a balance. He placed it on a table that another attendant had carried into the house. The king's agent placed the amulet on one side and gold weights on the other. The amulet ascended, then stopped exactly opposite the gold weights. The two sides were perfectly balanced. The eunuch then made a small streak with the loadstone on the inside of the amulet, and another on a small piece of gold he had taken from his pouch. He showed the agent the two streaks held side by side for comparison.

The agent scowled. "We have not yet detected your cheating. Remember, when we have, you will be killed."

Az bowed but, unobserved, rolled his eyes in disgust.

"The king has another task. He saw a circlet on one of the princes of Israel, the son of the captive Jehoiakim. You saw it no doubt when they were paraded through the streets at the festival of Shamash?"

"I saw it, Lord."

"The king desires one for his son. But in all things it must exceed that had by the Dog of Israel. It must be more ornate, more beautiful—in design more superb, in aspect more breathtaking, in character more profound. Do you understand? No son of a captive king will surpass our own beloved prince Amêl-Marduk!"

Az bowed again. "I will apply my humble talents to this request as best I can. I will not rest until his majesty is pleased."

The agent produced another bag and poured it onto the scale where the amulet had rested. There was much more gold poured into the cup than usual. The agent placed the counter weights on the other side. Almost two minas of silver! Az's wife could not help but look at her husband with eyes wide open. It was nearly quadruple the amount of gold he was usually given for a task.

"As usual, the king delights to honor his jeweler by paying in gold the same weight which he is asked to fashion." Az had taken the gold for the circlet and placed it in a leather bag. The agent then refilled the cup with gold coins until the weights balanced it yet again. Az emptied the cup into another bag, which he handed to his wife. She was smiling from ear to ear and had gone over to hug Az's mother.

"The king, our God, wishes his son to wear the gift for the celebration at the feast of Dumuzi. We will call again in two weeks time." The king's agent spun quickly and marched dramatically from the premises, followed by his lavish entourage. He did not stay to hear Az mutter coldly, "You honor me."

His wife hugged him. "Do you know what this means? We have enough for the place on the street of merchants. We will live upstairs! And your shop will be below."

He smiled. "It is true. This, with our savings, will be enough to buy it without question."

His son-in-law, who had been outside listening, stepped into the small room and said, "This calls for a dance!" He produced a pipe. Az's wife took a tambourine and, by hitting her leg, began finding the rhythm of the pipe. His two daughters and his mother began to dance around the room. Az joined them with a silver flute he had made while he was in Egypt. It was a joyous occasion. At last—to live among the rich and prosperous of the city—to find the recognition as an artisan he deserved!

3

MURUK LOOKED AT HIS FRIEND AND SIGHED, "YOU have a problem indeed." Muruk and Az had long been friends and seen more than their share of trouble together. They had grown up playing on the banks of the Euphrates; Az taking the part of Gilgamesh and Muruk, Enkidu. As children they had slain more monsters, tricked more gods, and defeated more warriors in battle than legions of heroes could have in a hundred years. Once they had floated down the Euphrates almost to Barsippa. It took almost two days to walk back, and when they returned their fathers had beaten them so severely—in gratitude to Ishtar for their return—that Az thought his father was determined to send him to Ereshkigal in the underworld. But this time the trouble was Az's alone.

"I warned you to stay away from metals. Did I not?" Muruk shook his finger in mock severity. A slave came and refilled their glasses. She was dressed in Egyptian linen and wore more gold than even Az had seen as the king's jeweler.

Az grimaced. "And I laughed when you said wool was the future after the fall of the Nineveh. By the king's beard! Look at you! You live like the king himself . . ."

"Better!" Muruk laughed.

"Better indeed! You have slaves that own slaves, and they wear more gold and silver than my wife can even imagine wearing! It's fortunate the king's gaze is away from Uruk or I'm certain the tax collector would be here in a bull's breath," Az said, shaking his head in disbelief.

"Bosh," Muruk laughed. "The king gets his share, I assure you. But there's still room if you'd just forget your 'art.' Wool is moving so fast I can't keep up. From Egypt to Greece the demand is high. I could use a good man fluent in Egyptian."

Az laughed again. "You never quit! No, my hands are my gift from God, not my head. But I did not travel all the way from Uruk to hear more of your bragging. Come, you promised to hear the dream."

"So I did. Leave out nothing if I am to interpret it. Even the smallest detail can be important." Muruk stroked his beard purposely and looked at his friend with a deep, wise look.

"The dream was even more clear last night. The thing is to be made of brass, the finest brass, like that produced in Greece. But though I can at least see the device dimly now, and its dimensions and aspect are becoming more clear to me each day, I cannot guess its purpose. And once made, what is to be done with it? One thing *is* clear. This dream comes from my God."

Muruk coughed and waved his hand impatiently, "My friend. I cannot interpret this dream unless I am told more about this new god of yours. I must admit you confuse me. You were Marduk's favorite. He has watched over and blessed you like few others. How do you turn your back on him in favor of this minor kingdom's deity?"

Az sat back and took a drink of the mead Muruk had set before him.

"You deserve the full tale. Sit back and listen—if you can manage not interrupting such a story."

Muruk waved him on and Az began. "I was returning from Egypt. Jehoiakim had just fallen and Jerusalem with him. The king of Egypt had just retreated past the great river and I was returning, along with several merchants, with some gold we had gotten at a great discount. War does strange things to a people's economy. We were well defended and several groups had joined ours to bask in the safety of our large confederation of Babylonians, Israelites, and Arameans. I needed some contracts written and I hired a Hebrew scribe to do some work for me. He was a smart fellow, but with a rugged edge that I liked—very Babylonian, if you follow me.

"We had some long conversations late into the night. We talked of great mysteries, exploring questions about the stars and their course through the heavens. One of his ancient prophets had written great things about the stars and their purpose in the heavens. In our conversations he made known that he was a scribe to another great prophet to this God of Israel. His name was Baruch—an able and well-mannered man, but devoted to this prophet like no scribe I had seen in Babylon.

"He told of how their God had taken them, as slaves of Egypt, and turned them into a great and mighty people through unbelievable miracles such as dividing great seas, or fire from the heavens, or fighting battles for them when they were outnumbered and faced sure defeat. Of course, I've heard such stories all my life, of gods mighty and terrible that raised a hero or a people to great heights of glory according to their whim and will, but no story ever touched me like the stories that this man told. It seemed my heart had caught fire and my head was filled with the light of a sun that seemed to shine within.

"After three days of such conversation, I decided that I would make an offering to this God when we arrived in Jerusalem. I told my plan to Baruch, thinking it would please him. Instead he just scoffed and said his God would not take such a sacrifice. This was not a God that one could satisfy with a sacrifice to appease or win His favor. This was not one of a pantheon of gods, but this was the One God. The ruler of all heaven and earth.

"I asked what he demanded and Baruch leaned over, looked me in the eye, and said, 'Your life!' I was taken aback and replied incredulously 'My life? He wants me to offer myself as a sacrifice?' Baruch had then laughed. He told me that no, not literally, but in a fashion, yes. This God demanded that I serve him and him alone, that my whole life and being be given for His purpose and for His glory. Then he told me something that struck my mind with such power that I wrote down the words. I still carry them with me, so let me quote them as I wrote them down fresh."

Az took out a small clay tablet that fit comfortably in his hand, then took a breath and continued. "He said, 'You asked if my God demanded you offer yourself as a sacrifice. No man can offer himself. You cannot offer your life, or another man's life, or even a thousand lives with any effect. But this God will do something that no god would dare do. This God—this God who created everything you see from the mountains that surround us to the stars you see in the sky—will offer Himself as a sacrifice for us. You see, this God is a son. The son of the Father of our spirits, and for us He will die. And He will do it for a reason that would be unheard of from the gods that you worship with their plans and schemes, with their petty jealousies and moods. The reason is love. This God will do it because He loves you. He loves all of us. Through his death we are redeemed. We will live with him forever!'

"I had never heard such words before—no, I say that wrong. I have never *felt* such words before. They penetrated every corner of my soul. I felt their truth as much as I feel this cup in my hand, or feel the seat upon which I sit. They carried me away and I felt the love of this God. I feel it to this day. This God who will one day die for me, I've come to know is real, more real than anything I've ever known.

"Well, my friend, to make a long story short, Baruch immersed me in water in the name of this Son of God, His Father and the Spirit, which carries the love and truth of this God. He told me that he held the priesthood of one of their great prophets—one Aaron. At that time I gave my life to this God and His people. I promised that I would always remember the sacrifice that this Son would make and in so doing I would find mercy for my own transgressions and I would find forgiveness." Az stared into his cup as he said these last words.

"Your tale strangely attracts me," Muruk said after a moment. "I find a comfort in your words and seem to taste some of the light you describe in feeling these things."

Az looked up and smiled. " I find I cannot speak of these things without feeling again all that I felt. It is that Spirit of which I told you in whom I believe. Yet there is so much I do not understand."

"Have you not spoken again with this Baruch? Has he taught you no more?"

"Sadly no. When we arrived in Jerusalem, events transpired that forced Baruch from me. His prophet, Jeremiah—my prophet too— has been imprisoned by Zedekiah and Baruch had to go into hiding immediately. He was entrusted with sacred writings that had to be preserved. So there is much that I have not learned. Yet, still, I pray and think upon the things that I learned. And now this dream comes again and again. I know that it is from this God—my God, but its meaning is unclear."

His friend refilled Az's cup. "Tell it to me. I have some skill in the interpretation of dreams. As you know, I was once consulted by one of the court astrologers on a dream of the king's." Muruk had leaned back and was looking rather proud of himself, raising his cup for emphasis.

"Yes, yes . . ." Az laughed. "That is why I've come to visit you. I thought you might help clear these muddy waters."

His friend leaned back and twirled his hand in the air saying wisely, in a deep voice and with an air of mystery, "Tell me the dream!"

"In the dream, I see a brass ball. Cut in half. It is covered with Market Egyptian . . ."

Muruk interrupted him. "Market Egyptian? Please, I must know everything. Explain."

"Yes—they use it for everyday writing. You've seen the glyphs of their walls."

"Of course."

"Such writing is too long and artful, so they have an abbreviated version to be used for everyday writing. Merchants use it quite a bit, hence, 'Market Egyptian.'"

"Yes, now I remember having seen it used. Can you read what it says on the ball?"

"No, but it is clearly Market Egyptian. The base of the ball, forming the bottom half, is perfectly round, and running along the inside edge of that bowl is a clear stone or glass that forms a rim around the inside. The center is dark, but rising from the ball are round, gilded bars shaped like the wings of birds. They rise and meet at a round hook like that on a lamp. The wings are narrow and you can see easily in between them into the darkness of the center of the bowl. The wings rise from the edges of the bowl, completing the sphere and giving the impression that the whole device is carved from a single ball of brass. It is beautiful beyond description. Attached to the crystal ring are windowlike frames that slide over the top of the rim. In these windows appear words of Market Egyptian that change and shift—the words seem to dance within the ball."

Muruk interrupted, "I don't understand this clear stone rim. Can you be more exact?"

Az picked up two bowls, one larger than the other, and set the smaller bowl into the larger. He then poured his drink into the larger bowl until the rim of the smaller floated even with that of the larger bowl. "See the space that forms between the two bowls?"

Muruk nodded.

"Imagine that rather than a space, there is a crystal or clear piece of glass filling that space. It is such in my dream. Attached to this crystal are the windows that hang over the moving rings, which rings run next to the rim of the bowl just as the space does. It is in the windows that the words appear."

"Are the wings that form the covering of the ball of any bird you know?"

"I cannot say. They look like any bird, but like the rest, fashioned from brass."

"Then what happens?" Muruk asked, stroking his beard meditatively—his eyes closed in thought.

"I seem to travel to a new place, or I'm brought to a new place. It is night in the early spring, deep in the dessert, and I'm surrounded by court counselors, both rich and wise beyond reckoning..."

"How many?" Muruk asked.

"I'm not sure . . . several." Az continued, "There is a star shining in the eastern sky, so bright the landscape looks as if it's under a full moon. But there is no moon. We are all staring at the star. The counselors seem to be consulting maps and ancient texts. Then one of the men turns to me and asks, 'What gift will you bring?' And the dream ends."

Muruk leaned back with an air of mystery. "I am ready to interpret your dream."

Az looked at him, a little surprised with how quickly Muruk had come to his insight. "Go on."

"The dream is one that will make you rich beyond your wildest wishes, or even that of your wife," Muruk continued with a wink. "This god of yours wants you to begin in the trading of brass. While not as valuable as gold or silver, I've been following some of the merchants coming through the kingdom and there is a very superior brass that is blended in Kosala, which lies east of here, as the bright star of your dream signifies by its lying in the East. This brass is as hard as steel and holds a polish almost like gold. If you were to travel there, as I see your god wants you to, and start trading, the world would be yours. You see the ball represents the world, a world made of brass. The Market Egyptian writing means that you should watch carefully our enemy's attempts to beat you to the market. Egypt will be your greatest competition. The wings of the bird of course mean that you should act swiftly, as in the flight of a bird. And the rich astrologers signify you will be as rich as a king!" Muruk settled back and folded his hands on his wide belly. "I have spoken."

Az shifted uncomfortably in his chair. "He wants me to become a brass trader? That's what all these dreams are about?"

Muruk did not answer right away. He was staring straight ahead and drumming thoughtfully on the table. He picked up his cup, but did not take a drink. He was looking at it closely, but did not seem to be looking at the drink at all.

"Muruk?" Az finally interrupted the stare to bring his friend back to the business at hand.

"Brass! Of course! Why did I not see it before? With the war with Egypt in full swing and brass becoming more scarce than usual because of the disruption of Phoenician shipping lines . . . Of course! Brass could be the next wool!" Muruk had jumped up and was pacing the room. Several slaves had jumped up to attend him, but he waved them off impatiently.

"Muruk. I'm not sure *that's* quite what the dream means . . . I think that it has more to do with—" Az did not get to finish his sentence.

"Nonsense. Of course. It's so obvious it's a wonder I did not see it. Brass! We'll make a fortune! Leave the details to me. You're not set up to launch a caravan to Kosala and I am. You back me with whatever gold you've got and I'll throw in the rest. I can guarantee you'll quadruple whatever you put in." Muruk continued to ramble and would not quit arranging and planning for the remainder of the afternoon. By the time that sun had fallen behind the shimmering waters of the Euphrates, Az had agreed to turn over his gold savings to Muruk who would in its place bring back the finest brass manufactured on earth.

4

THE RED ROCKS SHIMMERED AHEAD AS THEY WALKED solemnly back to Babylon in the dry heat of the spring sun. Az looked at his daughter walking easily beside him and at the six guards talking loudly with them. The king's guard! What a luxury. But then the king's jeweler must have his protection when he traveled, and even though the way between Uruk and Babylon was relatively safe, these warriors made the trip much more secure than it would have been. They were not happy of course and complained incessantly about not being at this battle or that battle, but most of these guards had passed their prime as warriors. Some had even served with the king in the battle against the Egyptians at Charkemish.

Az looked down at his daughter and she looked at him and smiled. He and Melon-Flower had a special relationship, and she was the only one in the family that had joined him in his belief in

Israel's God. But they had always been close. Since she had been a little girl, she had been fascinated with all that her father did in his shop. She had helped for as long as she could remember, first just sweeping and cleaning, but lately, now that she was twelve, more important things like preparing the kiln or helping pour the hot molten metals into their molds. She longed to learn her father's arts, but knew it was not the custom. When she was old enough she would be made a bride and assist her husband in whatever work he did, whether it was tending goats or conquering kingdoms. She thought it odd that her father had not yet chosen for her a husband. Her mother was pestering him constantly about it, but he had put her off time and time again. She was not sure if she should broach the subject with him, but she too was growing more curious. Her mother had married her father when she was fifteen and in a few years she would be that age herself. Some of her friends had already been betrothed to their future husbands. The walk was a long one and there was plenty of time to bring up a difficult subject.

"Papa?"

Az smiled at his daughter. "What is it, my Melon-Flower? Tired already of walking?"

"No . . ." She hesitated as she strung out the no. "I was wondering..."

"What were you wondering?"

She could not do it.

"What is Mama going to say when she finds out you've pledged the gold for the house mama wants just to buy brass in the kingdom of Kosala?"

Az laughed. "I will tell you what she will say. First she will call me a fool. Then she will curse her father for ever choosing me as a husband. Then she will start to cry, whereupon she will fall on the floor and cover her head with dust, declaring it the greatest misfortune she has ever endured. Then she will most likely throw something at me. Nothing of value of course, but something she thinks needs replacing anyway. Then she will not speak to me for a week. Neither will my mother, and neither will your sister. I predict we will enjoy great peace for a week or more."

His daughter's eyes were wide. "Papa! Will they not believe Uncle Muruk's interpretation of your wonderful dream?"

Az chuckled and then looked as his daughter kindly. "I don't believe Muruk's interpretation of my dream."

"You don't?" his daughter asked. "But why did you agree to purchasing the brass?"

"That was a sly business move, little Melon-Flower. You watch, after the sale of the brass we will triple our gold." Then he grew more solemn. "But more than that, I felt right about it. It's not why the dream was sent, but . . . I'm not sure. It just seemed the thing to do."

"Oh."

Ever since that trip to Egypt her father had said things like this. He seemed to follow an inner voice that guided him in ways no one understood. At least her mother or grandmother didn't understand, but she did. She had believed everything her father had said. And she was starting to understand what her father meant when he talked about these feelings. She had begun to feel things herself ever since she had started to pray in the name of the Son, the Creator.

Az looked down at Melon-Flower. "It's hard to explain. But I feel guided by something bigger than myself. I've never felt like this before . . ."

"Not even when you chose my name?" his daughter asked with just a hint of concern.

Az laughed. "Well maybe *never* is too strong a word."

"Tell me again how you chose my name! How you left the midwife and mother alone to wait for my birth, and you walked along the river and . . ."

Az smiled at his daughter and began thoughtfully, almost to himself, "It was very dry that year—the fourth year of a frightening drought. The Euphrates was just a trickle and all of Babylon was frightened. Even the great gardens were dry and withered. Everyone was afraid that we would not have enough food to last another winter. Many said that your mother having a baby at such a time was a bad omen. They said your mother was past her prime and that the baby would be cursed. They claimed that she should have eaten the mugwort root and rid herself of it. But she would not hear of it. She somehow knew it was a daughter, and despite the protests of our relations, she carried the child. It was a hard time. Food was scarce and expensive. What food there was, was sent to the army to supply the war. When I left your mother in her pains, the midwife said to me, 'Do not hope overmuch. This is the fourth birth I've attended this month and they have all been dead at birth. The gods have deserted us.'

"So it was with a sad heart that I walked along the banks of the Euphrates. As I walked along the dry sandy bed of the river, I spoke to the gods I worshiped before I discovered the One God. I asked the gods why life was filled with such sorrow. The once-lush reeds along the river were a barren, dry yellow and the ribbon of water that ran small and lonely through the center of the once great bed was thick and brown. I could have jumped across the water's flow with ease, for a small streamlet was all that remained of the greatest river north of the Nile. I was about to turn back when something green among the reeds caught my eye. I approached it with wonder for I had seen nothing green in ages. There, tangled among the dried rushes, was a melon vine, green and alive, unconcerned that around it lay nothing but dry devastation. On the vine I found a plump juicy melon as big as my head, and beside it was a beautiful, large, full and delightsome yellow flower.

"I took both and returned to our home. The midwife was gone, but your mother was sitting up on the mat. Her long, tangled hair and pale face were streaked with moisture, but at her breast was a fat little girl sucking contentedly. A smile graced your mother's face. She glowed so brightly the room seemed as radiant as if it were lit with ten lamps. I looked at you, then at your mother, and handed her the flower. She held it to her nose and breathed deeply of its cool moist scent. I looked at the flower and at you, so beautiful and full of life, and an overwhelming sense of rightness, of blessing, flowed over me. I felt that all was right and all would be right. 'Our melon flower,' I whispered, and so your name was born."

Melon-Flower was beaming brightly. "And the rains came that very week."

Az smiled. "Yes. The rains came that very week. Those strong feelings of rightness had not returned from that time until I found the Hebrew God. I find such feelings often now."

They walked in silence for a few minutes. He looked at his daughter and smiled.

"It's these feelings that forbid me to rush off and find you a husband!" he suddenly declared as if he had been reading her mind.

She frowned a little and he caught the disappointment in her eyes as she spoke. "But Father, I'll soon be old enough and you and Mother have the most wonderful dowry set aside. I should not be surprised if you could capture me a prince!" She had blurted it all out before she realized what she was saying.

"A prince!" Her father laughed. Two of the guards joined in and one turned to her father.

"I would make a fine match for your little flower. And I could certainly use that dowry." The others joined in, laughing, but Az was not amused.

"Silence! You dogs are to serve me as you would your king. Would you treat a princess so?" The guard was silent. "I thought not," Az finished. "Do not speak of such things again."

Melon-Flower could tell he was very angry and an awkward silence fell on the company.

Az let the soldiers fall behind a little and in a quiet voice turned to his red-faced daughter.

"I'm sorry, Melon-Flower, the thought of one of those odious men . . . just . . . just . . . never mind. Don't worry. I have been thinking much harder about your marriage than your mother would ever guess. Daughter, it may be in a year or two I will want to leave Babylon and set up shop in Jerusalem."

She was surprised to hear her father say so, but said nothing.

"I long to go to the Temple regularly to offer up sacrifices to my God. That is the proper place of worship. I long to learn more about the God that I've embraced. And, well . . . I would like to find you a husband among the Israelites. You are a believer after all. What do you think?"

She put her hand over her mouth. "Papa! Really?"

"Yes, I think so," Az continued. "Just have faith little Melon-Flower. I'm learning that this new God takes care of His own. I think He has something special in mind for your life too. Can you have faith, Melon-Flower?"

She nodded and reached over, putting her arm around her father, and the two marched along the road toward home in warm silence, each lost in their own thoughts.

5

Az's PREDICTION OF HIS WIFE'S RESPONSE TO HIS using the gold for her new home had been more than accurate. For two weeks she did not say a word. And now, after four months, his mother had finally started speaking to him, but her conversation was mostly about where she had gone wrong as a mother, and how she must have angered the gods to have a son that would treat her so. But after two weeks, life for his wife went on much as it always did. There was bread to make, clothes to mend, lamps to trim, gossip to be exchanged.

The king had been most pleased with the circlet made for his son and had commissioned Az to make a grander one for himself. Much to the jeweler's wife's satisfaction, their coffer of gold had begun to be refilled. And as it was, Az's favor in her eyes began to be restored; she was almost being civil to him.

The dream appeared almost nightly now. The center of the ball was finally clear to Az and he could see two flat spear-shaped spindles floating in the center. They floated almost on air, and although they floated freely, there was a firmness and steadiness in their movement that gave them a sense of purpose. He felt compelled to follow the direction in which they pointed—he deeply *desired* to follow them as if the realization of his greatest dreams lay in the direction the spindles indicated. But the star was unchanging; every night it glowed there in the night sky. And the question, "What gift will you bring?" haunted him continually.

The birds had just begun their morning chatter when someone yelling brought Az off his mat. As he tried to clear his head, he realized that the voice was calling his name. He stumbled from the room, throwing a robe around him as he moved to the front of the house.

"I'm coming!" Az yelled.

As he entered the center of his house, there stood Muruk. The king's guards had gathered at the front of the house and were crowded around the door, peering in to see what Muruk was singing about. For singing he was. As loud as a gong and twice as deep.

"Muruk! You're back!" Az was wide awake now and embraced his friend, giving him the traditional greeting kiss. "I was beginning to worry. You've been gone almost four months!"

"The best four months I've ever spent. And as for you, my friend, you are a rich man!"

By this time all the family had gathered into the room. Muruk reached into one of the bags and produced a large, round, yellow metal disk. It was as large as a plate, but was as thick as his thumb was long. It was obviously very heavy. He handed the disk to Az, who carefully turned it over and over.

"This is beautiful, Muruk. I've never seen such fine brass. It's wonderful."

"That it is, and I've sold most of it already. These are just a few I saved for you, the rest are being moved to a buyer in town."

Something about the metal seemed familiar to Az, but he could not put his finger on it. The metal captivated him, though. He had seen brass many times, but nothing so fine. This seemed more like gold than brass.

Az looked up and laughed. "Then you've doubled my money?"

Muruk looked down at the ground. "Well, no. I did not quite double it."

A tension settled over the room that seemed to gather around Az's wife and mother.

His mother spoke first. "Well, how much did you make? You've at least returned what he gave you, have you not?" His wife was trembling and his mother moved over to put her arm around her.

Muruk was staring at the floor and seemed a little ill at ease. "There are risks in any venture, and what with the cost of the caravan, moving the goods to and from here, unexpected losses along the way . . ." He paused as if afraid to go on. "So, considering all of that, I was only able to increase your money by . . ." Muruk seemed to let the sentence linger for much longer than anyone in the room could stand. " . . . by twenty-seven times!" he shouted at last.

No one said a word. Not even his wife hitting the floor with a thud seemed to move anyone from their statue-like pose. Finally, as his oldest daughter rushed to help her poor, fainted mother, Az found his tongue.

"Twenty-seven times? That's a king's treasure. Are you sure?"

Muruk laughed a deep, satisfying laugh. "I'm quite sure! That god of yours sent you a dream of dreams. Of course, my own portion was much more substantial, as I had more to invest, but indeed yours is twenty-seven times your investment and the brass you see before you. You are a rich man now!"

It wasn't the money Az was thinking of, however. It was not even of his wife who was just starting to wake. Staring at the exquisite yellow brass on his rough dirt floor, he recognized why it seemed so familiar—it was the brass of the dream. Then suddenly everything became clear to him. Like a flash flood, in his mind he saw instantly the overwhelming task he was to accomplish. He was to make the device that had consumed his dreams for these countless months.

6

Az's NEW SHOP ON THE STREET OF MERCHANTS HAD
attracted much attention, with its two guards posted outside
the door and its central location in the heart of buzzing Babylon.
And as the rumors of Az's wealth gained momentum, to have one
of Az's gold pieces had become a necessity for anyone of status in
the kingdom. Az now had more orders than he could possibly fill,
so he had hired two other jewelers, whose work he respected, to
join him. They were Hebrew, some of the artisans brought up after
the defeat of Jehoiakim, but he was disappointed if he thought they
would be interested in discussions about their God. They were even
worse idol worshipers than most Babylonians and had no interest
in discussing things of a more spiritual nature. But they were good
jewelers and they worked cheaply enough.

Az's wife and mother had never been happier. They now spent
their days shopping and buying bread rather than baking it themselves. They strolled the gardens of Babylon with the wives and
daughters of others whose wealth allowed access to the parts of the
city that were barred to the less worthy.

While they pranced through the city, however, Az was not
happy. Under his shop was a small room he had named his treasury. And among the gold stored for his use, and the use of those
he hired, sat an ingot of brass that haunted him like the demons
of the underworld he remembered from childhood. Day after day
it seemed to call to him as he fashioned the ornaments to adorn
the elite of the city. It whispered to him at night and haunted his
thoughts as he visited friends and entertained customers during the
day. His dream had become even more vivid—the polished brass
burned into his consciousness. When he awoke, the memory of the
dream seamed to sear its image into his soul. There was an urgency
about it and every day he swore that today he would begin work on
the device. But every day it seemed that something would come up
that demanded his attention, pulling him away from what he knew
was of far more importance. Today was no different. Just as his shop

opened and he'd intended to send a servant (of which they had acquired two since their move) to fetch the brass, in strode none other then General Amasis, commander, second only to the king himself.

Az bowed low. "Your Greatness. It is an honor for you to enter my humble shop."

Amasis waved off his kowtowing. "I've heard great things of you. I have a task, for which none but the king's own jeweler will do. My daughter is to wed and I would like you to make all of the ornaments she will wear." Amasis pulled from a satchel a clay tablet, upon which was written a list of bracelets, anklets, necklaces, circlets, and waist bands that would keep an army of jewelers busy for weeks. Az stared at the list and realized that it would be at least a month of hard work. Perhaps more. The thought of the block of brass in the treasury crossed his mind just for a moment before it was pushed out by the thought of providing a service to the great man that stood before him. Known as the king's right arm, this was a man of which legends were told. A man destined to become a god. A living Gilgamesh. Certainly it was an honor to work for the king, but here was a man after his own heart—a self-made man. This man had risen through the ranks and had distinguished himself in countless battles: Nineveh, Charkemish, Jerusalem, and on and on.

Az bowed low again after looking at the tablet. "I can think of no greater honor, but, time . . . when is the wedding?"

General Amasis laughed. "Soon. On the day of the next moon. I will celebrate her wedding to my second in command, General Nabû, on the day of the festival honoring the god that has watched over me since my youth and given me victory after victory. You have slightly less than a month."

Az shook his head. "Your Grace, please understand . . . that is hardly enough time."

The general's face turned a bright red, his eyes began to blaze in a way that sent a shiver down Az's spine. "Then you refuse!"

"No, no . . . of course not," Az stammered.

"Perhaps the king has an order before mine? *That* I may excuse." Amasis' face was as hard as a desert stone and his aged face looked strangely fierce.

"No. The king's requests have been light. No doubt because of the excellence of the spoils you return from your campaigns." Az bowed again. "I will do it. If my forges must be lit day and night. Your request shall be honored."

The great commander relaxed. Amasis was a man accustomed to getting what he wanted. "I will pick up the order the day before the wedding." Then he leaned over and added mischievously, "And I pay better than the king!"

As the general left and passed the two guards (who were standing at attention so tall and straight that Az could not help but smile) Az stared at the tablet and began shouting orders. There was work to be done and not a second could be wasted.

At the end of the third day, Az was so tired he crawled into his bed exhausted. The wedding ornaments were moving forward, but it was going to be close. As he lay on the edge of sleep it occurred to him that he had not dreamed of the brass since he had taken the general's order. Perhaps his God understood the obligations he faced. That night he learned otherwise.

Az dreamed he was in his forge. He was working on an anklet and was carefully tapping away. A man stepped humbly into the forge. He was clothed poorly, like one of the shepherds hired to watch Muruk's flocks. He wore no shoes on his feet and his long hair seemed windblown and tangled. In his hands he held a small leather purse.

"We are closed until the festival of Adad," Az said, not looking up from his work. The man did not move, however. He stood there waiting as if he did not hear, then replied softly.

"I have work for the king's jeweler."

Az looked up. "Didn't you hear me? We are closed. I'm taking on no new orders."

"I have a work for the king's jeweler," the man said softly again. Az stopped what he was doing. Despite the man's appearance his voice pierced Az like an arrow. Az put down what he was doing and walked over to the man.

"I am sorry. Your work will have to wait until after the festival of Adad. I have an order from General Amasis." Az expected the name of the general to explain everything. But the humble man remained unimpressed.

"I have a work for the king's jeweler," he repeated firmly.

"Are you more important than the general of all the armies of Babylon?" Az asked sarcastically.

The man finally seemed to understand. He looked sadly at Az and asked meekly, "Then should I find another? It is a matter most compelling... and urgent."

"I'm afraid you will have to. I am far too busy. If you will excuse me, I must get back to my work." Az turned and walked back to the piece he was working on for the general. The man stared sadly at him for a moment and then turned to leave. As he reached the door, Az looked up. The aspect of the man seemed so sad and distressed that Az called out. "I am sorry. If you come back another time, I would be pleased to help you."

The man smiled kindly and with almost pity in his voice answered, "I am sorry, too. By then it will be too late."

Az looked at the man as he retreated out the door, and as an afterthought called out, "Sir! What is your name?"

But the man was gone. Az looked out his door and there in the cold night blazed the star shining brilliantly in the dark sky. He heard a voice say softly, "What gift will you bring?" And then there was silence.

7

HIS WIFE, HIS MOTHER, HIS DAUGHTER, HIS EMPLOYees, even his servants all stared speechlessly at Az. No one knew what to say. It was clear he had lost his mind. Since no one had moved he repeated his words.

"Please prepare the forge to work with brass rather than gold. I am going to General Amasis to tell him I will not take his order. As a gift, I will give him those things that we have made already. But we will make no more."

His mother found her voice first. "Did you hit your head? Are you moonstruck? He will kill you. You'll be thrown into the king's dungeon! You can't tell a general like Amasis that you have just decided not to take his business. I don't even think the king would dare do that."

His wife started weeping. "Doomed. We are doomed!" she repeated mournfully between her sobs. She stumbled over to the hearth and scooped up a handful of ashes and poured them on head. Falling flat on her face, she continued to cry loudly. Az uttered not a word but quickly walked from his home.

As he walked, he reflected on the reply that Baruch had given when he had asked what kind of sacrifice the God of Israel required: "Your life." Today such a sacrifice might be required, but he could do nothing else. The disappointment of his God still rang in his ears from the dream. He would do nothing else until the object required of him was completed—if he still drew breath after talking to the general. He had not gone far when he heard a familiar voice calling from behind. He turned around on the dusty street and waited until his daughter caught up to him.

"Papa! Mother says you are going to die! Is it true, will the general kill you?" Tears were running down her face, clearing a path through the dust her hasty run through the street covered her in.

Az gathered her up in his arms. His own eyes filled with tears at the thought of not being with his daughter as she grew to womanhood—of missing choosing a husband for her and missing the grandchildren that she would bear. He held her tight and she asked again.

"Is the general really going to kill you, Father?"

He took a deep breath. "He may, but my God has given me a task. Perhaps He will protect me."

"It's about your dream, isn't it!" Her eyes lost their fearfulness and her look of terror was replaced with one of hope.

"It is, Melon-Flower. I must get to work on making the device in my dream." He said this softly.

"Then all will go well for you, Father. I believe in your God. He always watches over us. Father, the general can't kill you." She pulled away and began heading for home, but turned and, smiling broadly, added, "I'll go and say prayers for you."

If only he had the faith of that child!

His stomach felt twisted as he approached the general's palace, and his heart was beating so hard he could feel it throbbing in his throat. He gave the gatekeeper his name and waited while a messenger was dispatched to seek the general's will. Az was hoping the general would be too busy, or that he would be away on some errand of the king, or bathing perhaps. Anywhere, but at home and available. But he was to be disappointed; the messenger returned with instructions to take the jeweler to the general's table where he was dining with a few of his military advisors.

"Your Greatness," Az said simply, falling to his knees and prostrating himself as low to the ground as he could.

"Ah. Come in. Honored guests may I present the king's jeweler—the finest artisan in the world. He is making the trinkets for the wedding of your bride."

A large man dressed in the armor of a field officer stood and bowed back to Az. It was the general's son-in-law to be, Nebû.

"What brings you to my table, jeweler? Come have a bite of lamb. Have you finished your task already?" The general signaled for a servant to set a place at the low table. But Az raised his hands signaling that he did not have time.

"General . . ." Az took a deep breath. "I must decline the task you have given me. I have brought the names of several goldsmiths whose talents exceed my own. Please understand that is a matter of utmost urgency or I would never dare beg to be released."

The general simply stared at him like a man trying to understand the babbling of someone who has had his tongue removed. Az had fallen to his knees again and had lowered his head, but he knew the submissive gesture would do no good. He could tell from the change in the rhythm of the great soldier's breathing that his anger had been kindled.

"You are refusing an order from General Amasis!? Are you mad? I have been treated with more respect by the kings of Egypt!" Az cowered as he heard a sword drawn from one of the soldiers standing by the door. He stole a glance at the general and saw his face so red and twisted in hatred that he knew then that he would die. When the general finally found his voice, he spat, "Slay him." A guard moved swiftly to carry out the grizzly work.

Az looked to the sky and called out in a loud voice, "O God of Israel, if I am to be your servant, have mercy."

"Hold!" The general's voice boomed through the small room. The soldier stopped a few feet short of where Az was kneeling.

"Why did you call on the god of Israel? Speak swiftly." The general's eyes were still narrow but his voice had lost some of its edge.

"It is He that I serve. He has given me a task, that is why I cannot fill your order."

The general sat back down. "So, the god of Israel has called you into service. Tell me the whole tale. It may be that you will live yet. This god interests me. I have often thought of sacrificing a bull to him myself. Come sit. Have some wine, and if I believe what I hear, you will live. If not, you will die."

Az came and reclined at the table with the other men. He was given a bowl brimming with the most delicious wine he had ever tasted. Once seated he held nothing back. He told the general of his dream. He described the ball in great detail, the star, the strange holy men following the glowing portent, and then he told of his dream the previous night, his required journey to Jerusalem, his daughter's faith, his wife's love—everything he could think of to ease the mind of the general. When he was finished, the table was silent. Suddenly Nebu's voice sounded, cold and callous.

"I say kill him. Dreams?" He laughed harshly. "He must be made an example of. If our own people do not respect the might of the military, then how can we expect it from our enemies? Kill him."

The other guest had not been introduced to Az, but he was obviously a man of rank and position in the army. He looked coldly at Az and said derisively, "I agree. He was given a great honor and has spat it out like a dog. Slay him."

The general looked at his two advisors. He stroked his beard and said thoughtfully, "You are right, of course. He should die. But I will not go against his god. This god of our jeweler is more dangerous than we can ever guess. Never have the Hebrews lost when they are in the favor of this god. He has done wonders that make our gods look like simpletons. Not long ago the Assyrian king, Sennacherib, attacked with an army that could have crushed a hundred nations. While camped outside Jerusalem, the army was destroyed in a single night. Not by an army of men, but an army so terrible that the survivors told tales that would freeze a man's blood. The stories abound. This god is dangerous. Look at this man. He knew he would die coming here! But better to face death than the wrath of his god. No, I will not touch a man who has been called to a work by this god. I know this god's reputation well; every general knows the power of this deity. If the Hebrew fools had not thrown the prophet of this god in prison, I have no doubt that our forces would have failed in taking the city." The general turned to Az. "So better to face your death than the wrath of this god, eh?"

Az looked up for the first time. He considered the men standing haughtily before him, their cups filled with rich red wine that stained their teeth. Suddenly the thought of the humble beggar of his dream seemed more majestic and noble than a thousand of these men who thought so much of their power and honors of the world. He rose to his feet and stated simply, "It was not fear that brought me here. It was love. I love this God more than I love my life."

The men stared in astonishment. Gods were to be feared, cajoled, tricked, honored, or venerated, but loved? The thought was so new they could not even comprehend it. The general was the first to find his voice. "Would that I had a hundred with such courage as you have shown. Babylon would stand for a thousand millenniums were it so. Your god must have some great task for you. There is some great purpose in this. I can feel it. Perhaps you are to make this thing to free the prophet that Zedekiah keeps locking up and releasing!"

"Perhaps, but whatever He asks, I must do." Az returned to his knees again remembering his place. The general paced for a few minutes and seemed lost in thought. The other two men in the room brooded narrowly over the jeweler that seemed to have caused such emotion in their leader. The general sat down and stared into his goblet for quite some time.

Then he arose and signaled Az to follow suit. "I release you. I will find another jeweler. I am leaving for Egypt in two months to collect the tribute from Necho in Egypt and Zedekiah in Jerusalem. If you would travel with me, I would be happy to escort you on your task." The general extended his hand and Az grabbed his upper arm as the general grabbed his.

All Az could mutter was, "Thank you. I would be honored to travel with your eminence and the army of the king of Babylon." And it was over. It seemed amazing, as he walked the crowded streets of Babylon, that not only was he still alive, but he had obtained the escort of the greatest army on earth to travel to Jerusalem. Truly this God he worshiped was a powerful ally.

8

WHEN AZ STEPPED LIGHTLY INTO HIS SHOP HIS wife screamed in joy and flew over to him, throwing her arms around him and kissing his face, unashamed of the scene she was making. He returned her affection with a warm and grateful hug.

"Ha!" His mother exclaimed triumphantly, "I told you he would not go. My son may be a fool, but he is not that much of a fool."

Az roared with joyous laughter, "Mother! Would that every son had a mother that could make me laugh as you do. Of course I went!"

Everyone stopped talking and the place grew quiet. He went and was still alive? His daughter broke the silence. "I knew he would be fine. Our God was watching over him!"

"Yes, He was!" Az exclaimed. "And not only have I been released from the general's request, but he will escort me to Jerusalem when I am finished with my task."

His mother shook her head and began to chuckle. "You had deceived me. I thought you really had gone." She turned to the other members of the family and, shaking her head, said, "He did not go. He's having a little joke with us. And it would have worked too, if you had not added that part about the general escorting you to Jerusalem. Very amusing."

Az laughed again but did not try to argue with his mother. "Is the forge ready to handle brass?" No one said anything. One of the Hebrew jewelers he had hired looked at the ground and said, "We did not think you were coming back, and if you did, we thought it would be to complete the general's order."

Az was in too good a mood to be too unmerciful. The man's logic was impeccable; it was his faith that was lacking. "Then get to work, man, we'll be working only brass for the next month at least. We have a . . . a . . . something to make."

It was the best and worst month of his life. There were spiritual highs when he was sure the great God of Israel was guiding his hands and heart. There were days of such despair and despondency that Az was sure the task was beyond his skill. He allowed his employees a month of rest, with wages. He sent his wife, mother, and oldest daughter and her husband to visit with his uncle in Kish. Only his youngest daughter, Melon-Flower, who believed in his God, was allowed to stay and assist. Each day began with prayer. Az pled for guidance in making the device that would free His prophet, for surely that was what it was for. Ever since the general had suggested the idea that this strange ball could be used to free Jeremiah, the prophet of

Israel, Az had decided that must indeed be its purpose. Somehow, Az marveled, he, an obscure jeweler, was being called upon to free the holiest man on Earth. And he took his task very seriously.

Melon-Flower helped her father from morning till night. She worked the billows to keep the kiln blazing; she handed him tools; she cooked their meals and bought bread and supplies from the market. She did all this cheerfully with an air of fulfilling a mission and the sense that there was something very holy about the work in which they were engaged.

By the end of each day they were both exhausted, but slowly the object of Az's dreams began to take shape. Each night the Lord instructed Az through his nighttime visions, which had become very vivid and clear during this time, on each step of the process. It was like nothing that either father or daughter had ever seen; like nothing they had even imagined. Az watched excitedly each day as the object took shape. The basic design was a brass ball of perfect roundness. Around the equator of the ball ran a band of clear glass. Inside the lower hemisphere of the ball, within the ring of glass, were placed a series of nested rings made of thin brass placed one within another. Each ring slid within another smoothly and independently. In each individual ring were fashioned a set of windows of various lengths such that when the many rings were rotated, the windows would be arranged in a way to expose different parts of the innermost ring, which was without windows.

The nested rings were attached with rollers that allowed the entire ring to rotate smoothly and without a sound. Words in Market Egyptian were written upon the innermost ring. These Az placed in relief instead of carving them, which would have been infinitely easier. When different layers of the nested rings were turned, the windowlike frames could be moved in such a way that any combination of words could be exposed, depending on which windows were open to the most inner ring and which rings did not expose the inner ring. Through the glass, the exposed words written on the inner ring could be read through the windows. The words changed as the rings were turned, and as the window frames moved within the device they framed new word combinations.

Every word he chose to place on the inner ring had been given to Az by the Lord through His Spirit. Az made each word of gold, then fused it to the brass inner ring. The rings had to be placed in tracks so they remained securely attached to the bowl frame. It was demanding, exacting work. When the complicated assemblage was ready, Az capped the lower hemisphere with a thin plate of brass so the rings were hidden.

Atop the plate, which hid the concentric rings, Az placed two spindles. Of all the inglorious metals that could be chosen, the Lord had commanded one to be made of iron, but the other was of purest gold. The spindles sat upon a little post in the center of the device and were so perfectly balanced that they seemed to float in the air. He noticed that the spindle of iron seemed to favor a certain direction, but the one of gold turned freely—not so freely that it spun randomly, but firmly enough that with the most delicate touch it moved smoothly and easily, much like the inner rings that allowed words of Market Egyptian to be exposed on the side.

To top the lower portion, Az ornamented the ball with a tall lid of such enchantment that his daughter declared it the most beautiful thing he had ever made. He had to agree. For the top half he carved the twelve symbols of the tribes of Israel and the spreading wings of a seraphim. These he inlayed with gold. The lid rose to a peak and numerous thin lines were cut into it so the spindles were clearly visible. Then he sealed the rounded top onto the bottom half so that the spindles could not be touched. The effect was of a perfectly round ball with a band of fine, clear glass around the rim that exposed words in Market Egyptian, and a rounded lid ornamentally carved through which one could see the spindles.

It was late at night when father and daughter completed the device. It was strange that the Lord had provided no way to move the rings from outside of the ball to determine which words to expose. There also seemed no way to determine which way the spindles pointed. But despite these oddities it was a wonder to behold. For what purpose this was made he could not guess. It seemed such a beautiful and amazing work of art that he knew beyond doubt that he had not made it. It had been his hands, truly, his kiln, his Kosalaian brass, his Nimrudian glass, his tools, but the work was not his. His skill as an artisan was great, but it was not at this level—his mind could not have framed such a wonder. Other hands had used his hands. Another mind had enveloped his mind and created something far beyond his humble skill. He could only claim the same credit an anvil might receive for producing a king's crown. Truly this had been prepared by the Lord.

His daughter, in tune with his thoughts, fell on her knees and spontaneously began to thank the Lord for their blessings. Without a thought Az fell to his knees and joined her in pouring out his gratitude for letting them be a part of their God's grand designs.

9

THE GOOD-BYES HAD BEEN HARD. AZ'S WIFE HUNG ON to little Melon-Flower for as long as she could until Az had pulled her away. He understood. No one traveled on a journey of this length without the risk of never returning. His wife had tried in every way to persuade him to change his mind and leave the little girl behind, but he fully believed that her prayers had saved his life, and it was her faith and help that had made it possible for him to make the device. She would not be left behind.

No one else understood this journey's cause. Az's mother was convinced he had lost his mind. His wife just wanted things to return to the way they were before (but not before he had made his fortune with the Kosalaian brass). And it was hard to convince them of the import of the trip when all they could see was a small cedar box.

Both he and his daughter had wanted to show everyone the piece of work they had wrought together; they wanted to take it to the king and have it receive the praises of royalty. But something strange had happened the morning before his family returned. Father and daughter had left the device covered on a table in the foundry; when they returned in the morning it was just as they'd left it, except that inside the window the Egyptian message was clear: "Show no one."

Az immediately called his daughter to him, and there was a trace of annoyance in his voice. But Melon-Flower held her hands out and said innocently, "I never touched it."

He turned back to the ball. "Then how . . ." He never finished the sentence and his daughter's wide eyes betrayed that she was thinking the same thing. In that moment he had put it into a padded leather pouch, then placed the pouch in a cedar box filled with sawdust. He had allowed no one to see it. His mother and wife found this quite insulting, but he was firm. No one would look at it until it was shown to Zedekiah and he offered it in exchange for Jeremiah's freedom.

So now they were walking. The hot red sandstone lay as far as they could see. They walked in the rear of the army with several other merchants who had paid for the privilege and protection of traveling to Egypt with the Babylonian army. The talk was of the asking price of barley and wool, the buying cost of wax, the continued rebellion of Egypt, and the quality of Greek poetry and such things. Where Az would normally have joined them in their speculations and gossip, now he was full of anxiety and remained silent. He knew that he would eventually have to stand before Zedekiah, but how to approach this negotiation was going to be delicate. If he approached it badly, he could end up not only losing the brass ball, but his life and the freedom of the prophet as well. He would have to make Zedekiah think that he had some protection . . . Ah, that was it. He was the king's jeweler. He would say he wanted to show Zedekiah what he had made for the king, and that it was being protected by Nebuchadnezzar's army. Then, after the old puppet king had had a chance to lust after it, he would mention his conversion and his love of the prophet Jeremiah. Then he would offer Zedekiah the ball in exchange for the freedom of Jeremiah. That would be the approach to take. As long as Zedekiah thought Az was supported by the might of Babylon, he would not likely try to steal the ball.

But then, rumors out of the south seemed to suggest that Zedekiah was getting more rebellious, and though he had not turned his back on Babylon completely . . . the possibilities disturbed Az, something was bothering him, though whether it was his plan or something else he could not tell.

Perhaps I could find Baruch and consult with him. Az thought. *That is what I will do.* So on he walked thinking of meeting and freeing the prophet, meeting his old friend Baruch, and winning the praise of his God for the great work he had performed.

The journey took two weeks and was largely uneventful, but there was something magnificent about traveling with the greatest army in the world. Az stared at the soldiers marching around him, their bronze-plated armor scattering the sunlight. Except among the young recruits, few were without terrifying scars—their legs, arms and faces marked with the savage wounds of previous battles—giving them each a fierce, defiant countenance. Their peaked, conical helms rising to a point, their braided, squared beards, the metallic click of their swords, the soft thud of the butt of their spears striking the ground as they marched in laced sandals and linen kilts—all of this gave them an unconquerable demeanor that Az admired, and even envied. They carried provisions, as well as additional weapons like slings, bows, and arrows, with ease. Az was amazed that they could walk all day carrying the implements of war and apparently not tire (although he overheard not a few complaints from time to time). Ahead of the columns of foot soldiers rode the great cavalry, horsemen of rare skill and agility armed with bow and spear. These men were stern, proud, and daring. Az could not help but wonder what it would be like to face such men in battle. He suspected their visage alone was enough to put some enemy soldiers to flight. Az felt a strange longing to be a man of such caliber and strength. Most glorious of all, he thought, were the drivers of the great war chariots. Leading the cavalry, the chariots held the elite commanders, the lords, the princes, and the general's most trusted officers. The general himself rode in a chariot driven by four fiery horses, stallions strong and fearless. That well-crafted vehicle would allow him to drive from one part of the battle to another with great speed in directing the affairs of war. Surely there was nothing to compare with the army of Babylon!

Az walked in the rear with the merchants, the wives of the soldiers, and the logistical support of smiths, leatherworkers, carpenters, cooks, bakers, grooms—an army of people almost as large as the fighting force itself.

Among this group on the heels of the army appeared those Az considered the biggest danger on the journey. These were Greek mercenaries—a rough lot lacking the discipline of the regular army. They spent much of the night drinking, fighting, and looking for trouble in the villages through which they passed. Az was especially worried about his daughter. She was now almost thirteen and nearly of marriageable age, and certainly old enough to attract the attention of men of the type who attached themselves to the army for pay. But since Az was a guest of the general, the men seemed to treat them with a modicum of respect. Nonetheless, Az kept an eye on his daughter, never letting her out of his sight.

However, he was grateful for the army's presence. It was strange to be traveling this far and not have the usual worries about bandits, zealots, and the ilk that preyed upon traveling companies. A small group was almost certainly going to be attacked. Even a large caravan would sometimes fall prey to a large organized band of thieves. But with the army of Babylon as their escort, there was not a force on earth that could challenge them. Not one.

Az spent almost every night in the massive and luxurious tent of the general playing games and talking about religion, the gods, and philosophy. But these talks always seemed to return to the God of Israel. Az described his conversion, and almost every night the general probed him for stories of this God and His works. They were nights never to be forgotten. A power attended their conversations that seemed to cause the lamps to shine all the brighter. Az discovered the general to be a very learned man; he asked difficult questions that exposed the heart of almost every topic he explored. The strange thing was, Az seemed to be able to answer these questions and even provide insights that were far beyond his ability to provide. In this he knew he was attended by a power beyond his own. The God of Israel was truly sending His Spirit to help him.

One night, as they neared Jerusalem, the general seemed in a particularly distracted mood. Az arrived as usual just after the evening meal, and the general ordered a slave to set up the game board. Az thought the general seemed more quiet than usual, but dismissed it as he watched the twenty-square game board being prepared. Amasis despised the simple dice games played so often by the soldiers under his command. He was, however, a master at many of the more challenging games. He was not bad at Hounds and Jackals either. He had a beautiful set carved from jet-black obsidian and elephant ivory, which, he assured Az, was once owned by the current pharaoh. He was also very good at Kalaha and Senet, both Egyptian games, but his passion was the ancient Royal Game of Ur. At this Amasis was unbeatable. That's why, as the evening progressed, Az thought it strange that he was so far ahead of the general in the game. Az already had all seven of his pawns on the board, and had removed three of the general's without causing the usual deep frown or furrowed brow that marred the general's face when it seemed he was falling behind. Az was excited. He had four of his pawns on refuges and was starting to hope he might actually win his first game since leaving Jerusalem. He was going to beat the general!

But Amasis was rolling the sheep- and ox-knuckle bones distractedly in his hands and staring blankly at the board. Or rather, he was staring through the board. Something was wrong.

Suddenly, he looked up at Az. "You say there is just one god. One god who created the world. One god who rules the heavens. One god that makes the sun rise. One god who watches over the fates of nations. One god who brings in the harvest. One god to do all things. I find this impossible. Suppose you offend this god. To what other god do you turn? Suppose your sacrifices fail to please this one god? There are no options, nowhere else to turn."

The general paused for a moment and Az was about to say something, but Amasis continued.

"And not only that, suppose you are wrong? Eh? What then? If you sacrifice to several gods then at least there is a better chance that one will be able to help you. Before going into battle I always sacrifice to at least three or four gods, just to ensure I get the attention of at least one. Your faith is like a military commander that has put all his army in one place with a single plan of attack—with no chance to retreat, to call reinforcements, or to bring any flanking maneuvers into play. Placing all your trust in this single Hebrew god is not only foolish, but dangerous."

The general sat back and looked at Az expectantly. Az could tell it was his move and he chose his words carefully.

"You are right, if the choosing of gods is like a dice game. If it is just a matter of playing the odds, then your strategy is clearly the better. But suppose there is only one God. You have told me yourself of your impressions of the Hebrews' God. His prowess in battle. His destruction of Israel's enemies. He is a God of great miracles it is true, but He is more than that." Az paused to gather his thoughts. "I do not worship Him because of the miraculous events that I've seen—and I have seen many in my own life. No. I worship Him because He communicates with me directly. He guides my steps and opens the way for me. He is a God of not only large things like the courses of nations and the outcomes of battles, but He is a God of little things as well. A God who cares about my daughter's happiness as much as that of the kings and princes of Egypt . . ."

Amasis laughed out loud. "What kind of god do you worship? What? Does he care about the chamber pots and the contents of the cooking stove as well! Does he care about every straw in an old woman's broom? I have no use for a god of such minutia. Give me a god of strength. A god that embraces the virtues of courage in battle, of loyalty under command. Give me a god like Gilgamesh, the hero of old, not a god that fusses over the wishes and needs of a jeweler's daughter."

Amasis continued to shake his head and chuckle, but Az became earnest.

"You misunderstand. He cares about all of us not because He cares about the trivial . . . He cares because we are His children. His offspring. We are the sons and daughters of the Great Creator. We matter more to Him than the stars that spin above the earth, than the rivers, and the great oceans. We are His kindred. He cares about my daughter because she is His daughter as well. Do you see?"

Amasis had grown silent.

"That is why He cares about everyone. We are the children of this great God."

Amasis stroked his beard. "What a strange thought. You believe that everyone, even the most common beggar on the streets of Babylon, is in some way deity?"

Az waited while the general considered his words.

Finally the general smiled darkly. "I hope your religion never spreads far. That is a dangerous belief. What if everyone believed they were the offspring of a great god? Who could rule a people with such a belief? That would make a worthless beggar equal to a king. You keep this god. I will trust in a warrior's god who values a man by his strength, and who honors those who make themselves great."

With that, the general threw down the knuckle bones. Az lost two pawns and the game went downhill from there. Az lost again. But he left the tent humming to himself. Who would have thought that a simple jeweler would be playing games with the leader of the world's army, and on his way to visit a king no less; to visit a king in hopes to free a prophet. Az puffed out his chest and smiled as he returned to his own tent.

The days of debate and discussion passed all too quickly, and soon they reached Jerusalem. *At last!* Az thought, relieved. The city was much changed since he had visited before. Most of her artisans and princes had been taken north as captives in Babylon when she had been defeated by Nebuchadnezzar's army. The city seemed dirtier and less well kept since the defeat of Jehoiakim and the departure of her elite. A few merchants remained, along with some government functionaries—or those that fancied themselves such. But mostly the city was filled with the poor, those unfortunates that his king had not taken north. As the army passed through the gates, he thought of the Jerusalem that he had visited with his father when he was a youth. The markets had been full. The city seemed alive with silver, gold, wool and merchants. *What a change!* he mused. While Az looked about him, the general established his headquarters in Zedekiah's palace, and the army set up outside the walls, billeted in a tent city that arose within hours of their arrival.

Az entered the tent of the general to thank him. The general seemed preoccupied with his preparations to visit Zedekiah, but sent everyone away when Az entered the room.

"You have been a most intriguing traveling companion. I shall miss our conversations much!" The general was smiling and held out his arm for Az to grasp.

"I too will miss them. But, your grace, it has come to my mind that while you are here you should visit with some of the Elders of the Jews. They are much wiser than I and I think would answer your questions more satisfactorily!" Az reached out and took the general's arm.

"Perhaps. This god still intrigues me. One god. What a concept! It seems such a wasted pantheon, but the idea is compelling—if it were true." The general sat down and motioned for Az to follow suit.

"I have a request to make of you, Az. Perhaps I have no right, but since I have protected it—and since you made it on my time as it were—I would like to see the device before we part. I'm most curious to see this thing your God has had you make to free your prophet."

Az hesitated. He knew what lusts could be engendered by beautiful things, and here was a man who could take it with ease. Az also remembered the warning written on the device to show it to no one. But that was back in Babylon, did the Lord mean now too? He also knew to resist would end fruitlessly, so hesitantly, and with a measure of doubt, he reached into the satchel that had not left his side and pulled out the bundle wrapped carefully in sheepskin. He handed it to the general.

The general gasped when he had exposed the mysterious object. "It is beautiful!" The general turned it over and over in his hands, examining the writing on the sides and blowing on the spindles to make them turn. "Magnificent. I've never seen its equal."

Suddenly a change came over the general. Az could not be sure what it was: a narrowing of the eyes, a stiffening of posture, a tightness in the mouth? But whatever it was, he knew the general was not going to give the object back. The general set it on a wooden table and turned to Az.

"Jeremiah will be freed. I will see to it. Zedekiah is the puppet of our king and I am the king's fist. I will retain this device. Your mission is successful. It is unfortunate that we did not see this obvious solution before you had taken such a long journey." Amasis turned back to the ball and waved a dismissive hand at Az. "You may go. Your mission for your God has been successful."

Az remained where he was. Could the general be right? Certainly that is what he had believed was the purpose for making the device, but something seemed wrong. This was not the way it was supposed to happen; he could feel it.

"Your eminence, please. I do not think this is the way events are to transpire." Az stepped forward to retrieve his treasure. "If I may just take it and . . ."

In a flash the general had drawn his sword and stepped between Az and the ball. "Back, Dog! The thing is mine. You have fulfilled the mission your god gave you. Now go!" The general's eyes were firm.

"But . . ."

"Go!"

Az did not budge, but he was shaking. "My God forbids me." He stammered.

The general glared at him, but did not move forward. He looked back at Az and then moved toward the object resting on the table. "And *my* gods bid me take it!" And with that he reached out to pick it up.

What happened then was inexplicable. There was a flash of light as the general touched the device then was thrown as violently back as if he had been struck by the shield of a charging cavalry solder. The general stared in horror at the ball though it had not changed at all. There was nothing in its aspect that would have hinted that it contained such power. A moment passed in silence.

"Take it away!" the general said hoarsely. He was shaking violently. "Take it away! Your god has triumphed. Go! Go quickly."

Az did not hesitate. He gathered the ball—somewhat afraid to touch it himself—and its leather wrappings in his arms and fled the building.

For two days Az and Melon-Flower stayed at an inn near the Temple. The tension from the presence of the Babylonian army was palpable among the inhabitants of the city. Az heard rumors fly up and down the streets, rumors of help coming from the Egyptians, or that the Babylonians would be pushed back and Israel would be free. But Az's only concern was to find Baruch and ask for his wisdom and help in finding the purpose for his wondrous device. Would the general keep his promise after their less-than-friendly parting and free Jeremiah? Twice Az even tried to seek entrance to the palace to visit Zedekiah, and twice he was turned away. After two days the general and the army departed, but, to Az's delight and amazement, the general was true to his word—no doubt in fear of Az's God— and Jeremiah was freed from prison.

10

DID YOU SEE THE PROPHET, FATHER?" HIS LITTLE Melon-Flower greeted him at the lodgings they had taken in the great city. He gathered her up in is arms and swung her around and around until they were both dizzy and laughing.

"I saw him indeed!" Az exclaimed. "What a blessing. Daughter, it's true. He is a prophet. The Spirit taught me the moment I walked into the room. It was a not a voice like with which we speak, but it was so clear a declaration that I could not deny its reality. It was like something broke through to my soul and said, 'This is the prophet of Israel. He who holds all the keys for this day!' I can't tell you exactly how it felt, but it was real and it was from God."

Az sat her down and walked over to a small wooden table set up on the floor of the one-room dwelling that they had rented near the Temple. Az had spent almost every day at the Temple, making sacrifices, fasting and pondering over what to do with his glorious ball. On the table was a loaf of oat bread and some goat cheese. He sliced off a piece of both and walked back to his daughter.

"Will you say a blessing on this food? I'm ready to end my fast." His daughter offered a humble prayer then. Az dug into his meal with gusto.

"Would you like some wine, Father?" she asked, already pouring it into a brass cup.

With a full mouth Az mumbled his assent and had the cup emptied in a single draft. She let him finish his meal before she began to pester him with questions about the prophet Jeremiah. She knew he had arranged to see him and was anxious to hear if he had found out the purpose for the ball.

"He told me that the Spirit whispered to him that it was made for a great purpose—that it would serve as a symbol even until the last days!" Az mumbled in an excited voice with his mouth still full of bread. But then he lowered his head and added, "But he had no revelation about what was to be done with it. Clearly, at least, it was not to help release him from prison, for that's been done. But he said the Spirit was silent on its purpose."

Az's daughter nodded. "What should we do? Have you received any answers to your prayers in the Temple?"

Az shook his head. "No, though I feel very close to the Lord. Receiving a copy of the writings of Moses and Isaiah from Baruch has been wonderfully enlightening. Jeremiah is working on combining all the writings of the prophets into a great work, or I should say he is redoing it. He took all the writings from Adam to Moses and had combined them a few years ago and had them transcribed onto plates of brass, but they disappeared shortly after Zedekiah was placed on the throne. They were put in charge of a kinsman of the king's, but he was apparently murdered by a servant who stole the plates, and they have not resurfaced. The prophet is saddened but believes that they are not really lost.

"But all this is beside the point. He has started the redaction again and Baruch has given me a copy. It's wonderful! I must tell you the stories! There are stories about Adam, the first man, and his baptism; there is the rejoicing of Eve on our first parents' fall; there is the story of Moses seeing earths without number and of his terrifying battle with the evil one; and there is the story of the children of Israel being led from slavery in Egypt and of their coming to the promised land. It is fascinating, my child, just thrilling."

"Oh, that I could be taught to read," Melon-Flower sighed in frustration.

"You could learn, I've no doubt, were you allowed. But I will tell you the stories. They are wonderful." Az cut another piece of bread and pointed it at his daughter.

"My favorites are the writings of the prophet Isaiah. They tell of things to come at the end of our world and of the coming of the Son of God in the flesh. Wonderful reading my daughter—wonderful reading."

On and on Az talked, prodded on until late in the night by his daughter's questions. Together they read from the writings Baruch had given him until the lamp's oil was sputtering in the bottom of the bowl. When he blew it out and knelt upon the ground in the direction of the Temple, his heart was as full as it had ever been and he wept tears of gratitude for the things he was learning.

In the morning Az had a sudden thought that he should take the device with him to the Temple. His daughter was still sleeping so he left a little money on the table so she could purchase the night's meal, then he left quietly. The sun was not yet up, but there were people beginning their day; some making their way to the markets, some delivering goods to customers, a few making their way to the Temple, but few were going there to worship, he suspected. It seemed odd, but the people at the Temple did not seem to worship as he had learned from Baruch that they should. There were richly dressed priests who stood and declared the strength of Jerusalem and how it would never fall, and that their friends from Egypt would rescue them and that Babylon would be crushed very soon. The Temple was also filled with poor street vendors haggling for small household idols, some even for the worship of Baal, the old god Anu, who seemed to captivate these people more than their own God but was hardly worshiped at all in the rest of the world. True, the sons of Zadok were there sacrificing the doves and goats brought by the people, but the priests seemed rude and unkind, so unlike the God they were supposed to represent in the discharge of their duties. They seemed more anxious to receive their payment—something they'd recently begun exacting—than to help the people draw closer to their creator.

Jeremiah came once a day and preached to the people of the upcoming destruction of Jerusalem and their folly in trusting in the arm of Egypt for protection, but Az was horrified as his prophet—these people's prophet—was jeered and shouted down by the local priests and citizens. Jeremiah had wept sadly and talked of the coming destruction, but the people refused to hear him. Az could almost feel the hand of God hovering above them, but their eyes were blind and their hearts seemed closed.

But despite all this Az still came to the Temple. Despite the violation the great structure seemed to endure daily, there was a grandeur and magnificence that seemed to be calling the people to come back, back to the God that was once worshiped here in holiness and honor. It was here Az would find a quiet place in the outer court to pray and think. He was told that in former years he would have been closely questioned as to his worthiness, especially as a non-Hebrew and a Babylonian at that, but now he passed through courts without a single eyebrow raised in question. The Temple was indeed full of many foreigners, mostly sellers of objects of worship, or herbs and other things to heal the body or to free one of evil spirits and demons. There were also magicians and soothsayers. It saddened Az to think that this once great people, the very chosen of God, had stooped to this level of debasement. He shook his head and walked in sorrow. The voices of hypocrites surrounded him, and he realized this was not the people he expected to encounter in his newfound worship.

Az found a quiet place to pray and reflect on the far side of the outer court. There were a few humble beggars camped there, but it was not hard to find a place where he was largely undisturbed. He knelt and laid his burden on the ground.

"Show me the way, Lord," he pled. "Help me find some direction for your quest, some hint as to what should be done with this object."

As he prayed, Az suddenly felt very depressed. More so than he could ever remember feeling before. This quest suddenly seemed a hollow, worthless venture. His time and money had been wasted. There was no purpose to this thing, clever as it looked, as beautiful and wondrous as it was. It was a shallow, worthless thing—of no use to anyone. How could it be? Two pointers spinning uselessly in a gold-trimmed ball with Market Egyptian scribbled all over the side in moveable bands—it was a silly waste of time. He tried to pray harder, to make the feelings depart, but the heaviness continued and pressed upon his mind like a palpable weight. He had wasted his time. He had been tricked by feelings and dreams that were worthless and of no account. He had dragged his daughter through hundreds of miles of desert only to realize what a fool he had been! Dreams? Feelings? What were these to base such actions on?

Az started to cry and got off his knees. Sitting upon the ground, he stared at his hands. What was he doing in the fallen Temple of a poor and scattered people? Look how their God had left them—with a puppet king and most of the artisans and noble youth taken captive to Babylon. He looked at the bag of leather beside him. *I should just toss it over the wall and let it fall into the brook Kidron . . . No, I'll sell it!* Did not the general of Babylon lust after it enough that he was almost willing to slay Az? Perhaps he could offer it to the king. Zedekiah was known to have a taste for fine things. Perhaps he could get enough to trade for some things in Egypt.

But then he thought of the things he had read in the writings of the prophet Isaiah. Was not the condition of the Lord's people predicted there? He thought of his own feelings of hope as he sat day after day and read the sacred writings. He returned to his knees and said aloud, though in a meek voice, "My great God, in the name of thy Son who will come, even the God of Israel, please help me see clearly your plan for me. What is this thing I've made? Where should I go? Who should receive this humble gift that I've made?"

As he spoke a great calm filled his heart. The depression vanished as he mentioned the Son. Az opened his eyes and looked at the bag beside him. Instead of seeing a foolish, empty work, he saw a work of substance and purpose. He opened the bag and pulled out the ball. Written on the side were the symbols of Market Egyptian: "Well done, servant. Go." And one of the spindles was pointing south. He knew at last what he must do.

11

THE WIND TOSSED THE DESERT SANDS STINGINGLY IN their faces. It was the second such storm in two days, but Az counted it a sign he was going the right way. *If the forces of nature are combining to keep me from going this direction, it must be right,* he mused. But of course more important, the spindle had not failed him since leaving Jerusalem. It had pointed unfailingly the direction he was to take, and the direction was often surprising.

On the morning he was readying the camels he had purchased for their departure, Jeremiah and Baruch had stopped by, saying they felt impressed that he was leaving. The visit was short as

Jeremiah was leaving for Egypt in a few days and there was much work to complete on his sacred history of Israel. The prophet was still working on abridging and organizing the writings of Moses and had found a beautiful account of the creation he wanted to integrate into the text before he left. After saying good-bye, just as he was about to depart, the prophet turned thoughtfully back to Az.

"Would you like a blessing?"

Az was astonished. This was the prophet. "I would be more honored than I can express. Thank you."

Jeremiah placed his hands upon Az's head and, after invoking the great priesthood, spoke words of great comfort and satisfaction to the trembling Babylonian. Az was told that he was on God's errand and that as long as he remained true to the directions given him by the ball, he and his daughter would return safely to their home, no thieves or robbers would notice their passing, and the elements would assist them in unexpected ways. At the end of the blessing was a strange warning, so strongly communicated to his heart that he remembered every word:

"My son, you must have faith that the things you feel impressed to do are the things the Lord would have you do. Should you fail in this task or choose roads other than those you are directed to take, the promises given are revoked and you will be on your own, like a bird blown into the desert. Be true."

Indeed the blessing had been fulfilled in marvelous ways. On the third day out of Jerusalem they were passing a place where the road had passed through a narrow canyon. Az had been warned by several of the caravans that he passed that he would be a fool to pass there unprotected, but there was a sense of urgency in this quest, a feeling that he must press on and not wait for a larger party to join. As he entered the canyon, he saw a man standing like a sentinel near the entrance. He was dressed poorly and wore a large Egyptian-style sword. On his arms gleamed gold, and everything about the man spoke of danger. But as they passed, the man did not look at them once. The thief just stood staring off into the distance as if he had seen nothing. A few hundred leagues down the road a band of men of similar ilk were camped. They were playing games, practicing swordplay, and drinking. They looked savage and cruel. Az could hardly breathe as the camel upon which they sat plodded past this gang of thieves. Melon-Flower hid her face in the folds of her father's robes and hugged him tightly; he did not dare to take his eyes off the two camels they led behind them, which carried their supplies. They seemed to be making enough noise for a herd of camels. Suddenly two of the men playing a game looked up and stared at them. Az met their stares, knowing that the fear he felt could not be hidden. He almost spoke, but the men turned away and went back to their game. When they had passed Melon-Flower looked at her father. "I thought they would kill us, Father. I've never seen such horrible men."

Az looked down at his daughter. "Truly we are on God's errand. I thought they would kill us too. They would have—without a thought. But I think they did not even see us. Like the wind through a palm they may have felt the whisper of our passing, but they could not grasp it." He laughed out loud. "And what a treasure they missed!"

Az had just convinced himself that they were on the way to Egypt when the spindle pointed more southerly. There was no road going that way, and according to his knowledge of this part of the world there was absolutely nothing in that direction. It was wilderness, largely unexplored, uninhabited, and untraveled, and yet the spindle clearly indicated that it was the way to go.

"Well, daughter," he sighed, "this is our first test of faith. Do we go on and hope for a road heading that way, or do we just plunge into the wilderness? Our supplies are fresh from that last village. We have water for a week, but no more. What do you think?"

Melon-Flower looked scared. The wilderness was the place every city-dweller feared. It was a place of lions, ostriches, and other beasts conjured up in stories late at night, in particular for misbehaving children.

"I don't know, Father. Who could be down there? Why would the Lord lead us to a place where there are no people?"

Az thought for a while, then stood, dusting himself off. "I cannot even guess. Perhaps we will travel to the sea and meet a great king sailing the world. Perhaps we will find some nobleman from Enoch's departed city. I cannot guess. But the spindle says go, so we must go."

The journey now turned from the terror of dangerous men to the fear of wild beast, from the risk of robbery to a danger of hunger and of being lost, but the spindle led them on. It did not waver. For two weeks they traveled southward. The spindle seemed to lead them to every spring in the desert. They found plants to eat, and even a honeybee hive in the cavity of a lonely acacia tree. But even given these blessings their food supply was running thin and Az became worried. He reflected again and again on the words Baruch had first said to him about what his God expected: *Your life!* He was ready to give his life, but he regretted bringing Melon-Flower along. She was so young. Surely his God would not require her life. He should have left her in Babylon, or at least in Jerusalem. But it was too late, and on they wearily traveled.

The device pointed steadily ahead, never veering from the straight course it had set for them. The desert seemed endless. The sand, interrupted only occasionally by bare and wizened shrubs, seemed like an ocean of desolation. Even the camels seemed weary and plodded forward sluggishly. The animal skins holding their water had been squeezed dry that morning, the last few drops of their precious water failing to alleviate their parched throats.

"I'm thirsty," Melon-Flower complained quietly.

Az did not answer. He looked at her sorrowfully. Why had God taken them into this trackless waste? He felt a hollow depression settling over him. The sun was lowering and the desert stretched forward unending until it met distant hills in the horizon. His thirst was great and he felt hot, fatigued, and frustrated. He stopped his camel.

"What's wrong?" Melon-Flower asked. "We can't stop here. We've got to find some water."

"I don't think we can make it to those hills," Az said simply.

"Father, we have to. It's the most likely spot for a spring."

"I don't think this is the way it's supposed to be. We are following the Lord in everything. Everything! Didn't the prophet say the Lord would open the way? Remember the song that King David wrote? 'I shall not want,' it said. But this is too hard. I *do* want. I want water. We *need* water." Az seemed to be muttering to himself. "Everything about this is too hard. It seems to me that if we were really on God's errand, things would go smoother."

Melon-Flower climbed down and sat by her father. He could tell she was struggling too.

"Maybe we need more faith," she said guilelessly.

"Let's pray," Az said wearily. He lowered his head and asked simply that God bless them with water.

Both travelers opened their eyes and looked to the sky, fully expecting a dark cloud bursting with water to pour over them. The deep blue was unmarred by even a wisp of white. Az got up and explored the area, thinking that perhaps he should see if there was water nearby that they had missed. There was none.

Az sat down next to Melon-Flower. "We must be patient. We will wait here until we see the blessing and miracle of the Lord bringing us water."

They sat in silence for what remained of the day. When night fell they did not unpack the camels but sat in the shade of a rock, back to back, waiting. By midnight their mouths were so dry that they could not speak, and Az's tongue felt swollen.

Near dawn he looked at his sweet Melon-Flower, picked her up, and sat her on the camel's wooden saddle. He climbed aboard his own. His mouth was too dry to make the clicking sound that would move the camel forward, so he resorted to clapping his hands. The camels moved forward reluctantly.

Wordlessly they sat on the camels, rocking gently to the beasts' rhythmic gait. The day passed in a fog of semi-consciousness. Az had strange dreams. In every one of them, he was drinking, splashing and playing in clear, cool water. But when he woke up he was still suffering greatly from thirst. He looked over at Melon-Flower and it occurred to him that he should check on her, but the energy would not come, and he slipped time and time again into dreams of rich springs of cold water before he could finally bring himself to move.

Night had come. Through his mental fog Az thought it odd that they did not stop to make camp for the night, and vaguely wondered why they were still journeying so late, but the camels were plodding forward despite the darkness. Were they picking up speed? Strange. He slipped into another dream. In this one he was hanging over a cliff on a steep slope. Below him he could hear water splashing and strange slurping noises, but he could not see where the noises were coming from. In the dream Melon-Flower was calling him. "Father, water. Father, water." Suddenly something wet his lips. He sputtered in confusion, then drank deeply. Melon-Flower was holding a gourd to his lips. It was no dream. He had slipped off the camel and Melon-Flower was pouring a cup of muddy water into his mouth. Nothing had ever tasted better.

The camels were still drinking as he got his bearings. They were at a tiny spring where rich rushes grew around a pool of water no wider than the span of his arms. The camels must have found it on their own. Melon-Flower looked at her father and smiled. "God answers prayers." Az nodded, but he felt a little frustrated and he couldn't tell if it was because he had doubted or because the Lord had taken so long to answer their need. They had almost died. Wasn't there a better way to answer prayers? It seemed strange that the Lord would treat someone who had walked with generals and prophets so harshly.

They stayed two days at the spring and then continued their journey. After five monotonous days, tired and weary, they came to a valley which contained a small rivulet. As they looked down, they saw below them a nomad's camp.

12

FATHER, SHOULD WE TALK TO THEM?"

Az looked at his daughter and smiled. "I think we should. But let me check our marvelous ball to be sure. It would be nice to stop, rest, and talk and trade with them, but they may be dangerous. Remember, Melon-Flower, these are not the kind of people we want to stay long with. These wanderers are usually a dirty and unsavory lot, not at all the kind we want to associate with. And at all costs say nothing about our errand."

Az removed the ball from its leather covering. Strangely, the spindle was spinning as if the camel ride had loosened it. It spun slowly and then stopped, but Az had ceased looking at the spindle. The writing had changed! For the first time since leaving the Temple, the writing conveyed a different message. The words sent a shudder of disbelief down Az's back: "What gift will you bring?"

He stared in horror at the writing. What did it mean? Leave it *here* as a gift? Could the glorious star have portended this? Leave an object of such wonder and beauty with desert dogs? These people probably spent their lives wandering—poor and superstitious. These were nomads, beggars of the desert. What would they do with such a device as this?

He suddenly turned to his daughter and snapped, "Have you been playing with this? Was it dropped? I think you've broken it."

His daughter stared at him in surprise. "I've never touched it. It hasn't left the saddle bag since you took it out this morning to check the direction."

"Well, something is wrong with it!"

"Why?"

"Never mind. I'm going to get a closer look at these people. Stay here."

Az stomped off along the rim of the valley to get a better look. He backed the camels up so that they would not be seen and snuck as quietly as he could to a large rock near the camp.

The tents looked like they might have once belonged to a wealthy merchant, but they now looked weathered and worn. The people looked no better. It appeared to be only a small kin group consisting of three generations. An older couple sat by the tent door. The man Az assumed to be the patriarch appeared to be reading costly looking metal plates. His wife was mending. A younger mother was holding a baby and some young men were skinning a wild goat. *What a strange group,* Az thought as he looked down. Here was the patriarch reading a brass codex that looked like it was worth a king's fortune. One of the young men standing nearby, a large strong-looking lad, was wearing a sword that was of such beauty and worth that it even dazzled the jeweler's eyes. The hilt was of gold wondrously carved and ornamented; it was also richly inlayed with gems. Next to him was a bow of . . . *It could not be!* Az thought. *Steel.* Such metal was highly prized and the makers of such were a small and secretive group. How could such a band of wanderers obtain such treasures? Yet, other than these shows of ostentation, the group looked worn. Their clothes looked shabby from weeks of use and hung limply from their shoulders. Their animals looked thin and well-traveled and everything about the group cried out poverty of both mind and body.

Suddenly his suspicions of their lowness were confirmed. Several women gathered some of the meat from the butchered animal and began pounding it. After some time of watching this the patriarch called the group together and offered a blessing over the food—to what unknown god Az could only guess. After the prayer the members of this party began to eat the meat, raw. *Raw!* Az was horrified. His stomach churned within him and he fled back to his daughter.

"Get ready. We must go. We will not stop to share a meal with these swine. They are thieves. They have taken riches such as I have scarcely seen, and I'm sure they will do it again. Desert dogs like I've heard of all my life, and they are eating their meat raw. Come, let's go."

"Raw?" Melon-Flower made a face.

"Raw," Az repeated. "They look dangerous and well armed. Let's go quickly."

"Where, father? What does the ball say?"

Az picked it up, and to his horror, the writing had not changed and the spindle was firmly pointing at the family.

"It's broken. Something is wrong. Let's go back the way we came and camp again where we did before. We need to think."

Az was heavy-hearted as they walked back through the desert. It seemed impossible to move his feet forward. The Spirit that had so long accompanied him since the journey began was gone, and the heavy blackness they had felt at the Temple in Jerusalem returned. Every step forward seemed a burden. Even Melon-Flower felt it and she sat in the saddle silently staring ahead.

What gift will you bring? The thought echoed through his mind

That night they made a cheerless camp. Melon-Flower started a fire and they roasted some ostrich eggs they had found a few days before in the desert. Az thought about their trip; all the miracles, safety from thieves, fresh water, food as they needed it . . . all for what? Had it been a dream? Was his wife correct, had he been touched by madness?

Nomads! Why did the device quit working just then? Why not yesterday so he wouldn't be tempted into thinking that the Lord really wanted him to leave it there? Why did the words have to be something that made so much sense at that moment, but were clearly impossible?

Melon-Flower handed him his egg, but he could not eat it. His stomach was twisted in knots. He pulled out the ball and looked at the writing. It had changed, but the words were random and made no sense. The pointers seemed to meander loosely as if the ball really had been dropped. Az put it back in its bag and walked over to the fire.

"Father? What happened? I feel like crying and I don't know why. Those wanderers must have been wicked thieves. I have felt heavy and sad since we saw them."

What gift will you bring?

Az just nodded and returned to his own dark thoughts. *Should you fail in this task or choose roads other than those you are directed to take, the promises given are revoked and you will be on your own.* The words of the blessing echoed in his head. But he fought them.

What gift will you bring?

"They are vagabonds!" he said out loud. "They are nothing! This thing was made for a great purpose. It was made for kings, not beggars and thieves. I must have taken a wrong turn. I wasn't listening closely enough yesterday. That's the problem; we have to go back until the thing is working again. We have got to . . ."

What gift will you bring?

Az sighed. He knew what he was supposed to do. But it was too hard. Could everything he had dreamed about the device be wrong? Was it not made for a great purpose? This was not how the task was supposed to end—leaving the ball with strange and wild people. It was supposed to be given to a king, a prophet, or even an angel. Anyone but these nomadic wanderers.

What gift will you bring?

"Father." Melon-Flower spoke softly. "You were supposed to leave it there weren't you?"

Az could not deny it.

"Yes. I think so. But I cannot. I've been through too much. How can I leave it with . . . with them?" He waved a hand in the direction they had come. "It is too important to be tossed away like that."

What gift will you bring?

Melon-Flower looked at her father as his eyes filled with tears. She walked across the soft sand and picked up the bag and gave it to him. Az looked deeply into his daughter's eyes and nodded. He understood. This was not his mission. He was only the servant. He got up and dusted himself off. He stared at the stars shining above him and thought of the one shining in his dream. This would be his gift.

The round, full moon was just starting to rise above the horizon of the desert, casting long shadows over the rough terrain. Az patted his daughter's head with a sigh and started walking toward the nomad's camp.

"I'll be back by morning," he called over his shoulder and for the first time that day he smiled.

And it came to pass that as my father arose in the morning, and went forth to the tent door, to his great astonishment he beheld upon the ground a round ball of curious workmanship; and it was of fine brass, And with the ball were two spindles, and the one pointed the way whither we should go in the wilderness. (1 Nephi 16:1)

Bishop, Banker, Grocer, Fry

IT IS COLD IN THE SUBURBS. THE KIND OF SHADOWY chill that portends change. Bad change.

I should have known when Sister Dame walked into my office it spelled trouble. She came up to my desk and gave me that long look I feared as a bishop. That look that means my life is about to take a direction I'd rather it not take. But knew it would anyway. There are inevitabilities in the suburb, and I was about to meet one head on.

"Bishop."

"Sister Dame."

"I hate to bother you."

"That's why I'm here."

I take out a box of lollipops and offer her one. She pulls one out, toying with the wrapper like she doesn't know if she wants to suck it, or save it for a rainy day.

"I think my husband is into something bad."

"What's he doing?"

"I'm not sure."

I know where this is going. Husband overworked. Stressed. Starts looking for things to escape the cold, hard things the world throws at him. Gets started in things he can't stop. I hoped this wasn't the case. But I'd seen it often enough.

I consider Sister Dame. Sharp. Pretty. Calves that go all the way up to her modestly covered knees. The kind of woman you have to remind yourself not to look at twice—that you sort of wish you could be sick for, so she could bring you a casserole. Covered in foil. Hot from the oven. I pull my mind back. It's trending in directions I don't want it to take.

"Just give me the facts."

"Well, Joe's been working late."

"Yeah?"

"And leaving early."

"To the bank?"

"Yeah.

"Sometimes people work late."

"But it's different this time."

"Is it?"

"Yeah. It used to be when he worked he came home tired and sullen. You know, worn out."

"Now?"

"He's happy and chipper. Seems lighthearted . . ."

She stifles a sob. I hand her a tissue.

"I try to call him at his office. But he doesn't answer."

She lets out another sniffle. I hand her the box.

"Bishop, is there anything you can do?"

Something about this Sister Dame moves me to action.

"I'll look into it."

The next morning I'm in my car. Waiting for Joe to leave for work. Morning in Suburbia. Things are quiet. The sun casts a glow over the hustle and bustle masked by the houses lining the street. Times like this I forget that things aren't always as they seem, that the light rain that glazes the peaceful cul-de-sac's macadam will soon reveal the untamed terror of preschoolers tearing through the street on their Big Wheels.

Seven forty-five. On cue, Joe's garage door opens and he pulls out. A Toyota Corolla. Blue. I pull behind him, keeping a low profile. I feel a little silly and start thinking that following him is a mistake. Crazy even. I'm about to give up when he misses the turn to the bank. I hate when I'm right. I reach for my jacket pocket and pat the outline of my temple recommend book. I might not need it, but its presence comforts me just in case I do.

I follow him to a little store. You know the kind—a little Ma & Pa place that sells fresh fruit and vegetables. He goes in. I relax, thinking he's just going to grab something for tonight's dinner. I pull out the *Ensign* and settle in for a wait, but it goes on and on. He doesn't come out. I start to fidget and pull out a Tootsie-pop to calm my nerves. I know I shouldn't. I've been trying to quit. Refined sugar has been my demon far too long, but now is not the time to give it up. I need my guilty pleasures.

Joe's a good man. Far as I know anyway. I've never had a cause to worry about him. Suddenly I've got plenty. It's noon now and he's still in the store. My imagination runs away from me and I'm just about to go inside and scope things out when out he comes. He hops into the car and pulls out onto the busy street. I follow. He's not heading to the bank.

I follow him onto the Wicker Highway. Heading north. Out of town. I pull out another sucker. It's one of those days.

I keep my distance and almost miss him when he pulls into a diner off the highway. One of those 1950's mock-ups where people relieve the emptiness of suburban life by indulging their sense of nostalgia. I decide to follow him in. I have a job to do. If it comes to action, I'm ready. I enter and don't see him sitting in the long line of booths. He must be in the bathroom. I take a seat in one of the padded seats.

A waitress. Thick makeup. Tired. Dressed in white. Chewing gum. "What'll ya have, hon?"

"Cocoa. Black."

I drain three of these. Waiting. He still hasn't come out. I decide to see what's going on. The bathroom is empty. I run back out patting my pocket. A quick glance at the parking lot shows his car is still there. I rush to the back, hand on my temple recommend book. Then I see him. Sitting on the back porch. Taking a break. Dressed as a cook. He sees me and backs toward the door, thinks better of it, and faces me.

I'm nervous. Ready for action.

"Bishop!"

"Joe. What's going on?"

He lowers his head. "You got me."

"Got you what, Joe?"

My hand is twitching on my recommend book.

"I quit at the bank. Couldn't do it anymore. You know. It was stealing my soul."

"So here and the store back in town?"

"Yeah. I'm working two jobs."

"Your wife is worried."

"Yeah. I've got to tell her."

"You do."

"It won't be easy."

"It never is."

Acknowledgements

A NUMBER OF PEOPLE HAVE CONTRIBUTED TO THIS work. Stephen Carter edited the entire manuscript. Lisa Torcasso Downing, James Goldberg, Nicole Goldberg, Kristine Haglund, Eric Jepson, Heather Marx, William Morris, and Jenny Jones Webb have edited various stories from this collection and their help has been crucial (and since editing me is impossibly tricky, all the mistakes that remain are my own). I'm also grateful to the team at Zarahemla Books, Christopher Bigelow, Marny Parkin, Johnny Townsend, and Jonathan Langford. I am also indebted to my friends and family who graciously read these works and helped me refine them. Mostly, I'm thankful for my wife Lori who allows me the time necessary to stare out the window so these stories can be created.

About the Author

STEVEN L. PECK IS A PROFESSOR OF BIOLOGY AT Brigham Young University, where he teaches philosophy of biology and bioethics. His publishing history includes lots of scientific work—over fifty scientific articles, including publications in *American Naturalist, American Entomologist, Biological Theory, Biology & Philosophy, Newsweek, Evolution, Trends in Ecology and Evolution, Agriculture and Human Values,* and other science journals.

Peck's creative works include three novels. The magical-realism novel *The Scholar of Moab* (Torrey House Press) was named the Association for Mormon Letters best novel of 2011 and was a finalist for the Montaigne, a national award for the most thought provoking book. The existential horror novel *A Short Stay in Hell,* however, remains his most popular book.

Peck has published a collection of speculative poetry called *Incorrect Astronomy* with Aldrich Press, which includes the Science Fiction Poetry Association's 2011 Rhysling Award–nominated poem "The Five Known Sutras of Mechanical Man." He has also published in *Analog* (fact article), *Abyss & Apex, Black Denim Literature, Bellowing Ark, Daily Science Fiction, Dialogue, Glyphs III, Irreantum, Jabberwocky Magazine, Journal of Unlikely Entomology, Lissette's Tales of the Imagination, Nature Futures, Perihelion, Pedestal Magazine, Quantum Realties, Red Rock Review, Sunstone, Silver Blade, Sliver Thought Press, Tales of the Talisman, Victorian Violet Press,* and *Warp and Weave.*

44897971R00133

Made in the USA
Charleston, SC
05 August 2015